# SHAKESPEARE
## READERS



Volume 2

Othello

As You Like It

The Tempest

Much Ado About Nothing

**SCHOLASTIC**
New York Toronto London Auckland
Sydney New Delhi Hong Kong

Published by Scholastic India Pvt. Ltd.
A subsidiary of Scholastic Inc., New York, 10012 (USA).
*Publishers since 1920*, with international operations in Canada, Australia, New Zealand, the United Kingdom, India, and Hong Kong.



For information regarding permission, write to:
Scholastic India Pvt. Ltd.
A-27, Ground Floor, Bharti Sigma Centre
Infocity-1, Sector 34, Gurgaon 122001 (India)

First edition: October 2014

This reprint edition January 2026

ISBN-13: 978-93-5103-644-9

Printed at Shivam Offset Press, New Delhi

# CONTENTS

# *Othello*

William Shakespeare

**Retold by
Siddhartha Chakraborti**

## Characters

The Duke of Venice

Brabantio: *a senator*

Other senators

Gratiano: *brother to Brabantio*

Lodovico: *kinsman to Brabantio*

Othello: *a Moor, in service of the Venetian State*

Cassio: *his lieutenant*

Iago: *his ancient*

Roderigo: *a Venetian gentleman*

Montano: *Othello's predecessor in the Government of Cyprus*

A clown: *servant to Othello*

Desdemona: *daughter to Brabantio, and wife to Othello*

Emilia: *wife to Iago*

Bianca: *mistress to Cassio*

Other sailors, officers, gentlemen, messengers, musicians, heralds, attendants

# 1

Several centuries ago, in the city of Venice, lived a great captain who had a record of many victories. His name was Othello, and he was a Moor, but nonetheless he fought with all his might in favour of the Venetians, winning them many great victories against their enemies, the Ottoman Turks. Because of his victories, he soon became the most important and trusted of the captains who served the Duke of Venice, and rose to a position of great power and importance.

As his fame spread, he was regularly invited by important personages of the Venetian government to their houses for food and discussions. People were interested in this man, who despite being of a different race and colour, was the foremost defender of their city and its interests. Among them was an old and experienced senator named Brabantio, who had a daughter of peerless beauty—Desdemona.

Desdemona had many suitors, but her jealous father kept a strong watch on her. He ensured that she had fine education, that she was never found wanting in any way.

Although Desdemona refused all the young men who would come to court her, she was quite intrigued by the Moor.

One of Desdemona's suitors was a young man named Roderigo, who was madly in love with her. Roderigo had a friend named Iago, who was Othello's trusted flag-bearer. One night, Iago called to Roderigo to come out and meet him outside in the streets. He had fateful news—Desdemona had run off with the Moor.

Roderigo was upset and angry. 'How could this have happened?' he said. 'I hate you for not telling me about this earlier ... and all this while I thought you to be such a good friend that I even let you use my money as if it were your own!'

Iago assured his friend that he had no idea that Othello would run off with Desdemona, and swore that he hated his master Othello, and promised to help Roderigo like a true friend. He told Roderigo the reason for his hate. 'Three of Venice's most important noblemen took their hats off to him and asked him humbly to make me his lieutenant, the second-in-command. But he wants to have things his own way, so he side-stepped the issue with a lot of military talk and refused their request. "I have already chosen my lieutenant," he said. And who does he choose? A man who knows more about numbers than fighting! That man from Florence, Michael Cassio. He has a pretty wife but he cannot control her. And he has never even commanded men in battle. He has got no more practical knowledge of warfare than an old woman—unless you count what he has read in books, which any peace-lover can do. His military understanding is all theory, no practice. Yet Cassio has been chosen over me. My career is cut short by some bookkeeper, even though the general saw my fighting skills first-hand in Rhodes and Cyprus. This accountant is now lieutenant, while I end up as the Moor's flag-bearer.'

Iago bemoaned his fate, as being in military service in those days did not in any way guarantee promotion on the basis of service, but was merely based on favouritism. That is why he felt no loyalty towards Othello although he served him. But now he only served Othello to further his own ends. Having received no loyalty from the Moor, he felt there was nothing wrong in doing something for himself, while pretending to be dutiful and loyal in everyone else's presence.

Iago and Roderigo soon arrived at Desdemona's house. Iago then goaded his friend to incite Desdemona's father with the news of his daughter's elopement. They raised a big hue and cry. Brabantio himself came out to respond to the commotion. He shouted with all the authority of a senator. 'What is the reason for this horrible din?' Iago shouted back. 'Sir, you have been robbed. Your heart is going to break. You will feel like half your soul has been ripped out. At this very minute an old black ram is making love to your little white lamb. Wake up, wake up, get dressed and ring a bell, and wake all the snoring citizens. If you wait too long you will have black devils for grandchildren!'

Brabantio thought that some crazy men had disturbed his sleep, but he soon recognised Roderigo as one of the many men who were trying to woo his daughter. He thought maybe Roderigo had drunk too much and was creating a scene as a result. He admonished him, threatening to see to it that Roderigo was punished for creating a useless commotion. But Roderigo asked the senator to see for himself if Desdemona was sleeping in her room. Brabantio hurried inside, calling for light and raising an alarm in his household, fearing what he would discover inside.

Outside, Iago was in the middle of an explanation. He pointed out to Roderigo that while it was possible that the Venetian government would reprimand Othello, he was sure that they would not do away with his services, as he was needed to lead the Venetian army for the war which could break out against the Turks over Cyprus any day. So he could not be seen working openly against his master. However, a search party should be organised, Iago said, and mentioned that he would be with the Moor at the Sagittarius Inn.

Meanwhile, Brabantio returned, having discovered that his daughter was indeed missing. He ordered his servants to wake everyone and organise search groups. He even told Roderigo that it would have been better even if he had assented to him marrying his daughter. Roderigo for his part told Brabantio to get some armed men and follow him, as he knew where the Moor was. They left together gathering soldiers as they went, with Roderigo leading the way.

***

Iago, meanwhile, had gone to meet Othello. People were already opposed to the Moor, having learnt that he had eloped with a wealthy and beautiful Venetian heiress. Iago had successfully brought out of the citizens racially motivated reactions against the marriage of the dark Moor to the fair Desdemona. He now set to work again, this time to convince his master of his loyalty. In the process, he fought a man who was trying to harm Othello, stopping just short of killing him. Iago pretended to be concerned for his master, but Othello was confident that he would be defended by the Venetian government. He was undoubtedly the greatest general of Venice, and the duke himself was likely to intercede on his behalf. Secondly, he too was a prince and of noble birth, although not a fair-skinned Venetian. And finally, he would never jeopardise his own position and safety through such a bold escapade if he did not truly love Desdemona.

Soon, another group of people was seen approaching. Othello's lieutenant Cassio was at its head, on an errand from the duke himself. Cassio was worried. 'Many of the senators have already been summoned to the duke's palace.

The warships which have been out at sea defending Cyprus from the Turks, have been sending out messages. The duke wants to see you right away!'

Othello went to his room to get ready. Being a soldier, he could sense the urgency of the summons. Outside, Iago told Cassio about Othello's wedding to Desdemona.

Othello came back ready to meet the duke. Just then, Brabantio entered with his servants, some soldiers of the Venetian watch, and Roderigo.

Brabantio shouted, 'That's him! He is a thief!' Roderigo joined him, 'There! That is the Moor! Catch him!' Iago, pretending to be on Othello's side, challenged Roderigo to a duel. Othello however was calm. 'Put your swords away,' he said. 'They will rust in the dew.' He proceeded to reason with Brabantio. 'Sir, your age and status as a senator are enough to convince me to listen to you. You do not need to coerce me with swords.'

But Brabantio was not in a mood to exchange pleasantries. He accused Othello of putting a spell on his daughter, and keeping her in hiding. 'Anybody who has seen my daughter can tell you that a beautiful and happy young girl like her, who has refused to marry all the handsome young men of the city, would not run off with an ugly black man like you unless you charm her with dark magic. You are not an object of love but of fear. You have either tricked her, drugged her, or kidnapped her!' He demanded that Othello be forcibly arrested. But Othello refused to be drawn into a fight. He said, 'You have charged me with serious accusations. Please tell me how I can defend myself to your satisfaction, but I refuse to fight.'

Brabantio demanded that Othello be put in prison until the day of his trial. Othello told the senator that the duke had called on him, and as such, he would fail to fulfil his duties to the Venetian state if he obeyed Brabantio's orders. Brabantio accepted that it was better the matter were presented to the duke.

Brabantio was surprised that the duke was in a meeting even at that late hour, but he was sure the duke would be on his side. 'My cause is just,' he said. 'The duke and any of my fellow senators will take this grievance as seriously as if it were their own. If we allow offences of this sort, slaves and heathens will be our rulers!'

Soon the entire group was on its way to the duke's palace.

***

At the duke's palace, a heated discussion was going on, regarding the intelligence reports the fleet had been sending. The duke was worried about what the Turks were up to, and the reports did not inspire much confidence in him.

Soon a messenger from another ship came running inside the palace. 'I bring a message from Signor Angelo—the Turks are headed for Rhodes and not Cyprus!'

This news was greeted with scepticism. Rhodes was

much better defended than Cyprus. Then again, Cyprus was always more attractive a prize for the Turks.

Just then another messenger came panting in. 'Sir, the Turks sailed to Rhodes and have joined with another fleet! Now they have thirty ships, and are headed for Cyprus. Signor Montano begs you to send reinforcements immediately!'

Amidst the confusion, Brabantio and Othello arrived at the court. The duke, while sending out dispatches for help, welcomed Othello warmly, and was about to tell him about the crisis when he noticed Senator Brabantio. He exclaimed, 'Sir, I did not see you there! Welcome, welcome. Your knowledge and experience will be of help tonight.'

Brabantio was not interested in the defence of the republic that night; he had more pressing matters at hand. He broke down in front of the duke, saying 'My daughter! Oh my daughter!' with such force that everyone present thought she may have died. 'She is dead to me,' he continued. She has been tricked and stolen from me, enchanted by black magic spells, for she would not have made this mistake on her own!'

The duke tried his best to console Brabantio. He told him not to worry, and that whoever was at fault would be punished and that too to Brabantio's satisfaction. Brabantio then told everyone present that the person responsible for his grief was none other than Othello.

The duke asked Othello to defend himself. Othello

obliged. He declared that he was a simple soldier, and was not very good with words. While it was true that he had married Brabantio's daughter, the charges of sorcery were certainly false. Othello asked Desdemona to be brought to court. 'If she has anything to say against me, then you can not only fire me from my position as your general, but you may even sentence me to death,' he said.

While Iago and some of the attendants hurried off to fetch Desdemona, Othello explained how he had come to love her. He told them how, when as a guest at Brabantio's house, he would narrate stories of his life and the many adventures he had had, Desdemona would always listen with interest. She would feel sad when he told tales of woe, and express happiness when she learnt how he overcame his obstacles. Then one day she expressed something more, saying that if she had a friend like him, she would definitely love him.

Desdemona was asked to testify, when Othello declared, 'She loved me for the dangers I had overcome and I loved her because she felt for me. This is the sorcery I have used.'

The duke advised Brabantio to come to a judgement himself, since such a fine story would have won even his own daughter.

It was Desdemona's turn to speak, and she spoke of her husband in nothing but supportive terms. With due respect, she told her father that she had willingly accepted the Moor as her husband. Brabantio was surprised, and remained reluctant to give his blessing to the couple, and bemoaned the loss of his daughter instead.

The pressing military matters required Othello to leave for Cyprus immediately. Othello, despite being recently married, wanted to fulfil his responsibilities as a captain, and hence requested the duke to make suitable arrangements for his new wife. The duke thought she could remain with her father for the duration of the war, but Brabantio didn't agree, and neither did Othello or Desdemona. Desdemona said, 'When I married Othello it was because I wanted to live with him. Since I am a part of him now, I need to be with this soldier and share his honour and bravery. I would be miserable without him. Let me go where he is going.'

Othello also agreed, saying that he wanted Desdemona to be by his side. He assured the duke that her presence would not make him lax in his duties.

The duke reminded him of the urgency of the situation. Othello and his wife would board the ship by nine in the morning.

The night was almost over. Iago stayed back to collect the commission on Othello's behalf and joined them the next morning. As they all left to make preparations, the duke told Brabantio, 'If your son-in-law had the colour of virtue, he would be amongst the fairest of men,' and urged him to make peace with the new couple.

Roderigo and Iago were left behind, after all their scheming met with failure. Roderigo realised that he would certainly not be able to win Desdemona anymore, and expressed his wish to commit suicide. Iago urged Roderigo not to kill himself, and assured him that he was still his friend. He advised Roderigo to sell everything he had. Sooner or later Desdemona would surely get tired of the Moor, he suggested. Roderigo would be a rich person by then, and would be able to win her easily. Grief-stricken, Roderigo agreed to follow Iago's advice.

After Roderigo left, Iago smiled and thought to himself that fools like Roderigo who are so ready to part with their money could be used with ease. He remembered the widespread rumour that the Moor was having an affair even with Iago's wife, and assured himself that he would have revenge. He decided to use Cassio's good looks as a means to acquire his position as well as avenge his slight. He struck upon an idea. 'I have got it! Cassio is a smooth-talker and a seducer of women, and slowly I will impress on Othello that he is a little too close to Desdemona. Othello will soon start to believe me. I have no doubt that he will be as easily manipulated as an ass is led astray.'

# 2

On the island of Cyprus, a huge storm had threatened to blow even the fortifications away. During the day, there was a very strong wind, and the sea waves were the size of mountains. Braving this weather, a gentleman named Montano, along with two of his friends, went out to the shore to check if the Turkish fleet had arrived, hoping that the reinforcements from Venice would come as well.

However, it seemed as if the storm had destroyed everything. While the three friends debated whether the Turkish fleet was still out in the open sea, a fourth gentleman joined them with cries of victory. 'The war is over! One of our ships has just docked in the harbour with the news that the storm has reduced the Ottoman fleet to debris!' Montano wanted to hear more, and he soon got to know that Cassio had just sailed into the harbour, and that Othello himself was expected to arrive shortly.

Montano stopped worrying about the Turks and prayed for Othello's safety, the Moor being stuck at sea still, in such stormy weather. He said aloud, 'I hope Othello is safe. I have fought under his command and I know him to be an excellent general.'

Cassio also came up and joined the four friends, and together they looked out for Othello's ship. Soon another sail was seen, and Desdemona and Emilia, escorted by Iago, came ashore and reached the group. Iago's skill as a navigator of ships was commended, since he had brought the ship safely through the storm and the rocks, and in very little time.

Soon another sail was seen at the horizon. While the group waited for the distant ship to dock, Cassio and the others knelt in front of Desdemona and welcomed her to the island. Iago continued to pretend that he was a coarse and honest person. However, he secretly noted how Cassio continued to behave in a flirtatious manner, kissing his wife Emilia on her cheeks, while also holding Desdemona's hand. These actions were usually considered a gesture of friendship, but could easily be misconstrued as being guided by loose morals.

At that moment, trumpets announced Othello's arrival. Othello exclaimed, 'Oh my fair warrior!' and ran into the arms of his beloved wife. The couple kissed and rejoiced as he had made it safely through the storm. Othello and Desdemona left for the castle to celebrate their reunion, while Cassio was put on guard duty for the night, and Iago entrusted with bringing the luggage into the castle.

When Iago and Roderigo were left alone, Iago immediately began poisoning his friend's mind against Cassio. He pointed out the number of times Cassio had held Desdemona's hand, and how they had fondled each other's hands. Roderigo corrected him. 'It was not an advance, but a polite gesture of friendship!' But Iago had struck the right chord, so he continued, 'They were being lecherous! Such proximity is not innocent. Did you not see how close they stood, with their breaths merged into one? Roderigo, in the present situation, how long will it be before something of gravity actually transpires?'

Roderigo slowly became convinced of the impropriety of Cassio's behaviour, and agreed to pick a fight with him. Iago managed to influence him to believe that, had Othello not been in the picture, Desdemona would have fallen for Cassio.

Iago's intent was to bring Cassio down in Othello's eyes. He explained his plan to his friend. 'Cassio is angered easily, and may try to hit you. That is exactly what you need to get him to do. I can then stir up the mob in Cyprus against him. I will make the people so angry that they will only calm down once Cassio is removed from his position. To get what you want, you need to get Cassio out of the way.'

Keeping the plan in mind, Iago assigned Roderigo to do guard duty as well, as that would ensure a meeting with

Cassio. After this Iago left, musing on how to avenge the Moor for having slept with his wife Emilia. Suspicious by nature, he thought even Cassio may have been sleeping with his wife, and wished to take revenge on all promiscuous men.

***

Meanwhile, news of Othello's victory over the Turks was heard across the island, as the Moor urged everyone to celebrate by dancing, making bonfires or in whatever way they pleased. Then everyone was invited to the castle for a banquet to celebrate the marriage of Othello and Desdemona.

***

After the celebrations, Othello and Desdemona were to retire to their nuptial bed. But before they left, Othello entrusted Cassio with the responsibility of ensuring that no mishaps would take place, that the party would not dissolve into chaos, and that the guards would not get too drunk.

Iago however had wicked plans, and he provoked Cassio to drink heavily. 'Come on, Lieutenant!' he urged. 'I have here a jug of wine, and these two other gentlemen want to raise a toast to the dark General Othello with you. This is a night for celebrations!'

While Cassio was being plied with drinks, Roderigo had already drunk gallons to overcome his sorrow over losing Desdemona. Iago wanted the drinking to somehow lead to a brawl with Cassio at its centre.

Iago saw Montano amongst the drinking company and started talking to him, pointing to Cassio, describing him as a man with a drinking problem. 'He drinks like this every night before he goes to sleep,' said Iago. 'He will stay up all day and night if he does not drink himself to sleep.' Montano felt sorry for Cassio.

Despite being very drunk, Cassio remembered that he was in charge of the watch. He walked unsteadily towards the battlements, followed by an equally drunk Roderigo who was all ready to provoke Cassio to fight.

Soon cries for help were heard. Cassio, while chasing Roderigo, shouted, 'Ha! How dare you try to tell me about my duties? Come, I will beat you up!' Montano tried to intervene, but Cassio had already hit Roderigo. Roderigo ran, crying for help, and Cassio started fighting with Montano for holding him back, and injured him as well. Meanwhile, the night guard came running and raised an alarm. Othello, roused by the noise, hurried out to find out what was wrong and ordered for the commotion to end. 'How did all this happen? Have we all become as barbaric as the Turks? For heaven's sake, stop this brawling!'

Soon some semblance of order returned due to the general's presence. Othello turned to Iago and asked, 'What is going on here, gentlemen? Honest Iago, you look like you have something to say. Speak up and tell me who is responsible for this.'

Iago pretended to be reluctant, but after some coaxing, he informed Othello that Cassio had started the brawl with Montano, but suggested that there might have been some reason for it. By then Desdemona had also come outside to find out what was wrong. Othello saw that his wife's sleep had been broken because of the brawling, so he decided to be harsh. 'You are no longer my officer, Cassio! And let this be an example for everyone else!' He sent off Desdemona, telling her that a soldier's day was never over, and took Montano away to personally tend to his injuries. He knew it was important to make the Cypriots feel that he was not going to be partial to his own men. He needed to ensure he had their support in the face of continuous Turkish aggression.

Cassio was left alone with Iago. He bemoaned his fate and said, 'Oh, I have lost my reputation! I have lost the immortal part of myself, and what remains is merely an animal. My reputation is gone, Iago!' Iago consoled Cassio, but in his mind he was already plotting the next step of his revenge. Cassio regretted having drunk at all and failing the trust that had been vested in him. So Iago came to his aid and offered him a possible way out of his disgrace.

'Hear my suggestion,' he said. 'Othello is completely devoted to his wife and she has a lot of influence on him. Open your heart to her and ask her to counsel you about how you can get back your lost position. She is so generous and kind and ready to help that she will do even more than what you ask for. She can help you in healing the rift between you and her husband. Your problem will be taken care of, and your relationship with Othello will be stronger than ever.'

Cassio agreed to the plan since he was in such a desperate situation. Iago was happy that all was going according to plan. Now he had to ensure that Othello would see Cassio with Desdemona, and then Iago would be able to hint at a possible involvement between the two. Iago knew he would need his wife's help, so he left to set up the next part of his revenge.

# 3

The next morning, Cassio went to the castle hoping to meet Othello and convey his apologies. He took a troupe of bagpipers in order to wish Othello a good morning. But very soon, the clown in Othello's service came running out complaining that the nasal tone of the pipes did not impress the general. One of the musicians tried to enquire about the nature of the problem. The clown angrily said, 'Anyone who is full of hot air is a problem! If you can play music that has no sound then you may, otherwise go and vanish into thin air!' He paid them some money, and asked them to leave since Othello was not in the mood for music.

Cassio realised that Othello did not wish to talk to him and told the clown to ask Emilia to come out and meet him. Iago's wife Emilia happened to be Desdemona's handmaiden. Cassio wanted Emilia to help him find audience with Desdemona, so that he could get her to plead his case with her husband.

At that time Iago was passing by, and he told Cassio that he would not only send his wife Emilia out, but also get the Moor preoccupied with other things so that Cassio would have a chance to talk more freely with Desdemona. Unaware of Iago's devious plan, Cassio thanked him for being the most honest man of Florence.

Emilia came out to reassure Cassio that everything would be all right. She narrated how Desdemona was strongly arguing his case with Othello, and Othello himself wished to help Cassio as he liked and respected him very much, even though he had injured a very important man in Cyprus. Emilia asked Cassio to enter the castle, and assured him that he would find audience with Desdemona.

***

Inside the castle Othello told Iago to deliver some letters for the Venetian government to the captain of the ship which had brought him to Cyprus. Meanwhile Othello would inspect the island's fortifications. He told Iago to join him there once he was done with his task, and took some other gentlemen with him to make sure their defences were in place.

***

When Othello left, Emilia arranged for Cassio a meeting with Desdemona in the garden outside the castle. Desdemona told Cassio that she would do everything in her power to help him. 'You are my husband's friend,' she said, 'and you have known him a long time. I assure you, the only reason he is keeping away from you now is to appear politically correct.'

But Cassio was not satisfied. He said, 'I am afraid these political considerations may last a long time and the general might forget about my love and service. What if I lose my job and am sent away, and someone else takes my place forever?' Desdemona assured Cassio that she would not allow that to happen, and would continue to plead his case with her husband.

Othello and Iago had by this time returned from their tour. Desdemona asked Cassio to stay while she spoke to her husband. But he left when the Moor said that he would feel even more uncomfortable if he was seen trying to make his case through Desdemona.

Cassio's meeting with Desdemona did not miss Iago's sharp eyes. He said aloud, 'Ha! I do not like this!' Othello asked Iago what he meant. The Moor noticed Cassio as he was leaving. Othello asked Iago, 'Is that not Cassio?' 'Cassio, my lord?' Iago replied. 'No, I don't think so. He wouldn't sneak away with that guilty look if he saw you coming.' In spite of himself, Othello felt jealousy and suspicion creeping into his mind.

Desdemona was blissfully unaware of these thoughts in her husband's mind. She told him that someone who was currently in disfavour with him had asked her to speak on his behalf. She revealed that it was his lieutenant Cassio, who had just left. He wanted to beg the general's forgiveness. 'Dear husband,' she said, 'if I have any influence over you at all, please forgive him. In my opinion, this man respects you a great deal, and his mistake was out of naiveté rather than wickedness. Please call him back.' But jealousy was brewing inside Othello. He dismissed the suggestion and muttered something inaudible under his breath.

But Desdemona persisted and asked for a definite date when Othello would meet with Cassio. She reminded him of the time before they were married, when she would be angry with Othello, and Cassio would always take his side. She asked her husband to help Cassio like any old friend should. Othello did not look too happy, so Desdemona scolded him. 'Do not behave as if you are doing me a favour! You make such a big scene even when I ask you to do something that will be good for you. If I ever have to ask you for something that will make you undergo hardships, I wonder how terrible your reaction will be!' Othello gave in, and consented to Desdemona's request. But he begged to be left alone for some time. Desdemona left with Emilia, while Othello stayed with his malicious friend.

Iago immediately fuelled the fire of jealousy already burning in Othello's mind. The general was too numbed by the thought that his wife had been disloyal to him to question Iago's motives. Besides, he believed Iago to be a straightforward, honest sort of person. On the one hand

Iago told Othello to be wary of such emotions as jealousy, but on the other hand he suggested, 'Keep an eye on your wife, observe how she behaves with Cassio. Do not trust blindly. I know the people of Venice; they will take your trusting nature for granted. Since you are not from around here, let me tell you that their motto is not to do no wrong, but rather to make sure that no one finds out that they are doing something wrong.'

Iago continued, 'Desdemona deceived her father to marry you. So is it not possible that she could be deceiving you now to be with someone else?' Othello admitted that while he did not think Desdemona had been unfaithful, there was always a possibility that she might be in the future. Iago egged him on by pointing out the racial difference between him and his wife. 'She must have deep-seated desires to not be with a dark Moor, but a fair Venetian. Keeping this in mind, you should not restore Cassio to the position of Lieutenant right away. Wait and see if Desdemona presses you for it, and if she does then you should consider yourself right for suspecting her of having feelings for Cassio!'

Iago now left Othello to plunge into sorrow. 'A Venetian lady would surely want fair, handsome men in the spring of youth,' he thought. Just then Desdemona came back with Emilia to find out what was taking Othello so long. Seeing him sitting alone and distressed, she pulled out her handkerchief, which Othello had gifted to her once, and said, 'You must have a headache for not sleeping too well these last few days. Let me wrap this around your head, and you will feel better soon.'

Othello refused her help, and dropping the handkerchief accidentally, went into the castle with Desdemona.

Emilia picked up the handkerchief, remembering that Iago had wanted her to steal it from Desdemona for quite some time. She had no idea why, but she gave it to him anyway. What Iago intended to do was plant the handkerchief in Cassio's apartment and have Othello discover it there. He was sure that this could be passed off for concrete evidence of his wife's infidelity.

Othello was indeed finding it difficult to feel at ease. He demanded proof from Iago and threatened him with dire consequences if he failed to prove the terrible allegation he had made against Desdemona.

Iago said that he could provide circumstantial evidence. He recalled how once he had been lying in bed next to Cassio, and how Cassio had murmured 'Sweet Desdemona! Let us be careful! Let us hide our love!' Then he had held his hand tightly, thinking Iago was Desdemona, and said, 'O sweet creature! Curse my luck that you should be with the Moor now!'

Othello in his excited state believed Iago's words. But Iago was yet to unleash the handkerchief. Feigning innocence, he asked Othello, 'Have you seen a strawberry-spotted handkerchief in your wife's hand?' 'Yes, it was my first present to her,' said Othello. 'Well, it may have been,' Iago continued, 'but today I am very sure I saw Cassio wiping his beard with that same handkerchief.' Othello said that if that was true, then not only Cassio, but even Desdemona deserved death.

Iago meanwhile pledged his allegiance to the wronged Othello, who gladly made him his new lieutenant. Iago was assigned the task of killing Cassio within three days, and Othello took on himself the task of finding a way to kill his wife, who he referred to now as 'the fair devil'.

***

Meanwhile, Desdemona went to wake Cassio up, and ran into the clown. Desdemona asked him, 'Do you know where the lieutenant is lying?' The clown, finding an opportunity to engage in wordplay, replied, 'I would not dare accuse a soldier of lying!' But he promised to go and find Cassio for her anyway.

Desdemona had meanwhile noticed that her handkerchief was missing, and mentioned that to Emilia.

Soon Othello returned and Desdemona reminded him of his promise to reinstate Cassio as his lieutenant. Othello, wearied by the thought that his wife had been adulterous, changed the subject. He pretended to have a bad cold and said to her, 'Can I have the handkerchief I had given you?' But Desdemona ignored him and continued to press Cassio's case, but Othello took this to be a further sign of her undue interest in him. He informed Desdemona that she must find the handkerchief as it was a magical one, made by an Egyptian witch. According to this witch, the woman who owned the handkerchief would have the power to make her husband like her always and be by her side forever. He told her that it once belonged to his mother, and he had saved it for his wife so that she would always be as faithful to him as his mother had been to his father.

Desdemona was taken aback by the sudden ferocity with which Othello had spoken. So she changed the subject again and asked for Cassio to be reinstated. At this Othello swore at her and left.

Emilia wondered about the inexplicable jealousies that seemed to seize men. She tried to console Desdemona, saying that it was perhaps some pressing political urgency that was making Othello behave in a disgruntled manner.

Meanwhile Iago came, dragging Cassio with him, asking him to present his case again to Desdemona. Desdemona tried her best to cheer Cassio up, and then hurried away with Emilia to try and find her handkerchief.

Meanwhile a local prostitute, Bianca, who had had her eyes on Cassio for some time, came to try and entice him. Cassio apologised to her for his continued absence, and gave her Desdemona's handkerchief to make a copy of the design since he liked it very much. He said, 'I found this in my room. I must return it to whoever has lost it.' He had no idea that it belonged to Desdemona.

Bianca wailed that Cassio was interested in another woman, but he assured her that it was not true. 'I am waiting here for the general, and I must not be seen with a woman. Please leave me now, and I will make it up to you later.' Bianca left, carrying the handkerchief with her.

# 4

At his castle in Cyprus, Othello was deep in conversation with Iago. Iago was slowly polluting Othello's mind with thoughts of Desdemona and Cassio being happy and intimate with each other. Othello believed him without investigating the truth himself.

Iago was not one to stop, so he brought up the handkerchief again. Othello writhed in pain and jealousy and accused Iago of polluting his mind with thoughts of his wife's infidelity that haunted him like a nightmare.

Iago suggested, 'What if Cassio has bragged about lying on your wife in bed?' Othello could bear it no more. 'I will hang him and then draw forth confessions from him!' he said, fuming with anger.

Iago watched with satisfaction as his words slowly poisoned Othello's mind. Finally he called out to him. 'My lord, do you hear me?' As luck would have it, Cassio walked in at that moment. Seeing Othello so enraged, he asked Iago, 'What is the matter?'

'My lord seems to be having some kind of fit. He had one the day before and it's attacked him again,' replied Iago. Cassio suggested Iago rub Othello's temples, but Iago pointed out that the general seemed to be recovering from his fit. 'If I interrupt him now, he might froth at the mouth and his condition may worsen. Look, he is moving. Why don't you withdraw yourself while he recovers fully? I will talk to you alone later.' In this way, he managed to get rid of Cassio.

'My lord, have you hurt yourself in the head?' Iago asked Othello. 'May I request you to face the situation like the strong man you are.' Feeling betrayed, Othello cried out, 'A man who has been cheated upon in this fashion is no longer a man. He is reduced to a monster, a beast.' He begged Iago to fetch him a confession from Cassio, so that he could legitimise his anger and jealousy.

Iago then told him of Cassio's visit when he had been in his trancelike state. 'I made an excuse on your behalf and asked him to come back later so that I can talk to him alone,' said Iago. He requested Othello to calm down and listen to their conversation without revealing his presence. 'I will make him tell me the entire story of their liaison again. I will also try to find out when they plan to meet again.' He cautioned Othello not be carried away by rage and do something foolish.

After Othello went to hide, Iago mulled over his plan. He decided to talk about Bianca, the prostitute who doted on Cassio. Cassio would not be able to control his laughter while talking about her, and that would drive Othello mad. 'Given the state he already is in,' Iago calculated, 'he will easily think Cassio's laughter and gestures are in relation to Desdemona.'

Soon Cassio arrived. Iago greeted him, 'Hello there, Lieutenant.' The use of his former title made Cassio feel worse, and he expressed his desire to get his position back. Iago carefully replied, 'If you have Desdemona speaking on your behalf to the general, you will soon have your old job back.' Then he softly added, 'If you had assigned this job to Bianca it would have been done in no time.' Cassio sighed at the mention of Bianca's name, and hearty laughter followed.

Othello heard the men laugh, but Bianca's name, almost inaudibly spoken, missed his ear. Othello's jealousy drove him into a state of uncontrolled rage. Meanwhile Iago continued to heap compliments on Cassio for his manly triumph over a woman, which made Cassio laugh all the more. Othello continued to misunderstand the situation and his anger grew.

'So, I hear you two are going to marry,' said Iago. 'Do you take me to be stupid?' replied Cassio. He spoke at length about how madly Bianca was in love with him, but he did not mention her name once. Iago gestured to Othello to come closer and hear Cassio boast of his conquests. Othello did, and thought Cassio was bragging about the charm he had worked on Desdemona. In his rage, he misinterpreted every word Cassio spoke.

While Cassio was busy bragging, Bianca arrived, waving Desdemona's handkerchief at him. 'Liar!' she shouted. 'You told me that you had found this handkerchief in your room and didn't know who it belonged to. But you cannot get away with your lies anymore! This piece of cloth surely belongs to some other lady friend of yours, who gifted it to you as a token of her love. I do not want to have anything to do with it!'

Othello gasped when he saw Desdemona's handkerchief in Bianca's hands. Bianca stomped off angrily. On Iago's insistence, Cassio ran after her.

Othello came out of hiding, his blood boiling, with only murder on his mind. Iago instigated him further. 'Did you see your wife's handkerchief?' he asked meaningfully. 'And did you hear the way he was talking about her? He casually gave away Desdemona's gift to a whore!' Othello's anger knew no bounds, but he still pined for Desdemona. But Iago sternly asked him to forget about his unfaithful wife.

Manipulated, Othello claimed that his heart had turned to stone, and he would kill his wife and punish her for betraying him. Othello was torn between his love for Desdemona and his hatred at her betrayal, unaware of the mind games that Iago was playing with him. He remembered her sweetness one moment, but the very next moment he cursed her.

Knowing Othello's weaknesses well, Iago pretended to be compassionate and reasoned with him. 'If you are so affectionate towards her, why don't you accept her in spite of her infidelity?'

Reminded of her betrayal, Othello's rage resurfaced. He roared, 'How dare she cheat on me? I will chop her into a thousand pieces!' He asked Iago to get him some poison so he would be spared the pain of arguing against her arresting beauty. 'Do not poison her, rather strangle her on the bed she has contaminated with her betrayal,' said Iago. He offered to kill Cassio himself, and encouraged Othello to do what his heart desired.

Suddenly the sound of trumpets came, announcing the arrival of Lodovico from Venice, who had come on the duke's behalf. Desdemona and Lodovico came to greet Othello along with the attendants. Lodovico conveyed the duke's message to the general. Lodovico exchanged pleasantries with Desdemona, his cousin, and asked him about Cassio's whereabouts. Desdemona apprised him of the situation, begging him to fix the rift between her husband and Cassio.

Othello was only pretending to think about the duke's message. He was actually listening to their conversation about Cassio. He could not help but express his displeasure aloud, although each time he did so, he quickly pretended to be engrossed in reading the duke's letter. Both Lodovico and Desdemona were utterly confused by his behaviour and assumed that his anger was a result of the letter's contents. 'Maybe the letter has upset him,' said Lodovico. 'I think it suggests that he go back to Venice and appoint Cassio as Governor.'

Desdemona expressed her happiness out loud, as it also meant that she would be going back to her own homeland. This proved to be the last straw, and losing his temper, Othello struck her in everyone's presence, accusing her of being a shameless infidel. Lodovico was astonished at such behaviour and promptly asked Othello to apologise. Instead, Othello hurled more abuses at his startled wife and ordered her to disappear from his sight. Shocked and hurt, Desdemona wanted to leave, but Othello called her back to insult her further. Unable to bear the unfounded insults, Desdemona ran away, leaving behind a Lodovico surprised beyond his wits.

Turning towards him, Othello said that he had read the letter and would comply with its orders. He would return to Venice and reinstate Cassio to his post. Once again Iago cleverly used this opportunity to his advantage and spoke ill of Othello and elaborated on his vices, portraying him as a regular wife-beater, astonishing Lodovico even further.

***

Othello was interrogating Emilia inside the castle. 'You have seen both Cassio and Desdemona together. How could you not have suspected anything?' Emilia was honest and fearless in spite of the mad rage she was faced with. She only feared for her husband. She said, 'Why would I suspect anything? I saw no harm in their friendship. They never appeared to be doing anything wrong. They spoke aloud, never keeping their voices low. They never even sent me out of their way on any pretext.' Emilia pleaded with Othello to believe that Desdemona was an honest woman, willing to put her own life at stake. She cursed the person who had implanted this evil thought in Othello's mind and proudly claimed, 'My mistress is the epitome of chastity. If she is accused of infidelity, the purest of wives would be reduced to mere nonentities.'

Othello asked her to fetch Desdemona, and then lost himself in his musings. He could no longer trust his wife or anybody else who spoke of her innocence. It had come to a stage when for Othello, Desdemona's every action seemed to be hiding the secret of her unfaithfulness. When Desdemona came with Emilia, Othello fondly asked her to come near him and look into his eyes. Desdemona was taken aback by this sudden show of love when her husband had struck her just a while ago.

Othello asked Emilia to leave, ordering her to keep a watch at the door. As Desdemona pleaded with him to tell her what was troubling him, Othello said, 'Why should I? What do you think you mean to me that I should share my thoughts with you?' 'I am your wife,' cried Desdemona. Othello continued, 'Go ahead and swear it on God, because you will be damned to hell for swearing a lie in his name. But I forget how good an artist you are, although even the devils might mistake you for an angel!'

Desdemona kept swearing her innocence, but every time Othello retorted with an accusation. He shouted at her, asking her to leave, but Desdemona did not miss the tears welling up in his eyes. She still laboured under the impression that it was the duke's letter that had brought about this rage in Othello. Desdemona felt crestfallen and guilty. 'Believe me, sir, I had nothing to do with the duke's order,' she said. 'If you suspect my father in this regard, know that even I have lost all my respect for him.'

But Othello could not be pacified. He could bear the marks of poverty or slavery, sickness and sores, but he could not bear being reduced to a laughing stock by his wife, who had not only rejected him but also polluted herself by engaging in sexual liaisons with her husband's lieutenant.

Sensing Othello's anger, Desdemona asked, 'I hope you know that I am completely faithful to you. Have I done something to displease you, dear husband?' In response, Othello abused her by calling her a whore. Desdemona swore on God that she was being accused wrongly. But nothing she said or did could pacify Othello, whose anger was now beyond reason. Calling Emilia into the room, he handed her some money and put her in charge of locking up and keeping a watch on Desdemona.

Emilia was troubled herself to see Othello in this mad state. Her mistress was beyond any consolation. She neither had any answers, nor could she weep out loud. She was too ashamed to discuss her marital troubles with Emilia. She merely asked Emilia to lay her wedding sheets on her bed that night and requested her to bring Iago. She wanted his opinion on what she might have done to displease her husband.

As Iago rushed forth, donning a look of concern, Desdemona broke down completely and asked him if she indeed deserved the treatment Othello had given her. When Iago feigned ignorance about the entire matter, Emilia explained the developments that had taken place. Desdemona cried, 'Do I really deserve such harshness, Iago?'

Emilia was beginning to suspect that somebody else had meddled in the matter.

'I do not think anybody could go to such depths of evilness. It is impossible,' claimed Iago. Emilia started hurling abuses at the crook who she thought was defiling her master's mind, only to be scolded by Iago to keep her voice down. Desdemona begged Iago to suggest her a way of winning back her husband's love. 'I could never do what he is accusing me of! Believe me, my friend,' she pleaded. Iago consoled her and said that Othello was weighed down by the business of the state, and was therefore being irrational.

Just then the trumpets announced dinner. Iago asked Desdemona to stop crying and have some food. He promised her that everything would be sorted out in no time.

Roderigo appeared as soon as Desdemona left with Emilia. He had started to feel suspicious that Iago had made him a false promise of helping him win Desdemona. 'You seem to be making little progress in the matter, and have provided me with no opportunities to win the woman I love. You took away those jewels from me, promising me you will use them to entice Desdemona. But nothing has happened to that effect. I feel as if I have been cheated. So I will now directly go to her and convey my feelings. If she returns my jewels, I will apologise to her and take them back, and never bother her again. If she claims ignorance about those jewels, I will take you down in a duel,' threatened Roderigo.

Fearing that Roderigo would do exactly as he had warned, Iago immediately changed his tone. He said that such show of guts on Roderigo's part had impressed him. He also insisted that he was doing everything in his power to get the two of them together. He claimed that he was almost on the verge of success, and that Roderigo's desires would be fulfilled the following night, failing which he was free to stab Iago to death.

This was enough to stop Roderigo in his tracks. Iago took this opportunity to tell him about the orders from

Venice—that Cassio was to be deputed in Othello's position in Cyprus. 'Othello will leave for Mauritania with his lovely wife Desdemona, if this comes to pass. So the only way to stop him and prolong his stay is to kill Cassio,' said Iago. He informed him of Cassio's dinner plans with Bianca, and asked Roderigo to nab him on his way. Both of them left in search of Cassio.

***

As Lodovico bid goodbye, Othello insisted on walking him out. He looked much more composed than before. Turning towards Desdemona, he said, 'You may go to our room and wait for me; I will be back shortly. Send Emilia away for the night.'

Emilia was surprised to see him suddenly so composed and gentle. But she was also a little surprised that she had been asked to go on leave. However, Desdemona did not want to displease him any further. She told Emilia, 'Give me what I should wear for the night, and do as he says. That might abate his anger.'

Emilia's suspicions were growing. She wished that her mistress had never met Othello. But Desdemona was too much in love with her husband. She admitted as much. 'I love him even when he is so harsh with me; I love even his frowns and his anger.'

Emilia put her mistress's wedding sheets on her bed just as Desdemona had requested. Desdemona sighed. 'If I die before you do,' she said, 'wrap me up in those sheets, Emilia.' Emilia gently chided her for being so silly.

Desdemona was in a pensive mood. She sat down to tell Emilia the story of her mother's maid Barbary. Barbary was in love, but her lover left her. There was an old song she knew, which reminded her of her own story. She died singing it. 'I cannot get that song out of my head tonight. All I wish to do is hang my head down in despair and sing it like poor Barbary.'

Then they conversed about various other things, but the song kept coming back to Desdemona. She started singing it:

*'The poor soul sat sighing by a sycamore tree,*
*Sing all a green willow.*
*Her hand on her bosom, her head on her knee,*
*Sing willow, willow, willow.*
*The fresh streams ran by her, and murmured her moans,*
*Sing willow, willow, willow.*
*Her salt tears fell from her, and softened the stones;*
*Sing willow, willow, willow—*
*Lay by these—*
*Willow, willow—*
*Prithee, hie thee, he'll come anon—*
*Sing all a green willow must be my garland.*
*Let nobody blame him, his scorn I approve ...'*

But she stopped short, realising that was not how the song went. Every brush of the wind against her door made her feel that somebody was knocking at the door, but Emilia consoled her gently. Remembering the rest of the song, Desdemona began again:

*'I called my love false love but what said he then?*

*Sing willow, willow, willow.*

*If I court more women you'll couch with more men ...'*

It was already late, so Desdemona asked Emilia to leave as per Othello's order. For one last time she called her back and sadly asked, 'My eyes itch severely, Emilia. Is it a sign that I might soon be weeping?'

Emilia consoled her again. Desdemona asked her if there were really women who cheated on their husbands. Emilia replied in the affirmative and agreed that even she would be like them if she had the opportunity. Desdemona was horrified to hear this, and said that she would never be able to do something so terrible.

Emilia assured her mistress that if a wife did go to the extent of cheating on her husband, the fault would be her husband's, not hers. Desdemona, too much in love, refused to see any reason in Emilia's words. She bid her goodnight and prayed that she would avoid following such bad examples.

# 5

Iago managed to convince Roderigo of the advantages of killing Cassio. Both of them waited, hidden behind a wall on a street in Cyprus, as Iago further instigated him. 'Do not fear, Roderigo, for this will certainly improve our future. Stick your sword in him as smoothly as possible. I'll wait right next to you.' Roderigo, reluctant to do the murder, murmured encouragement to himself, 'Nothing to be worried about … I just have to kill one man. And then I will have everything I have always wished for.'

Iago on the other hand was busy reflecting on his own actions and their apparent outcome. 'Roderigo has been rubbed raw like a pimple that is ready to burst,' he said to himself, 'and now, whether he kills Cassio or Cassio kills him, either murder will work in my favour. Although it is Cassio's death that would prove more favourable for me. I hope he is the one that dies.' Hearing Cassio's footsteps, he hushed up, while Roderigo struck him with his sword.

But Cassio had armour underneath his cloak, and the

blow fell flat. In an attempt to defend himself, Cassio drew his sword and stabbed Roderigo. At this moment, Iago stabbed Cassio on the leg from behind, almost crippling him, and escaped. Hearing their cries, Othello reached the scene and saw Cassio in great pain. He felt honoured that Iago had gone to the extent of murder just to help a friend. He decided to follow his example and turned his attention to Desdemona. 'Now that your lover Cassio is dead, it's your turn to die. I have removed you from my grieving heart and will punish you for your lustful infidelity,' he said aloud. Then he left, fully prepared to kill his faultless wife.

Lodovico and Gratiano, who were nearby, heard panicked voices crying for help. But it was dark, so they thought it was probably a trap and decided to return with a bigger force. At that moment, they saw a man coming their way, with both light and weapons in his hand. It was Iago who came and asked them, 'Whose voices are those, crying out murder?'

Gratiano and Lodovico recognised Cassio's voice. Cassio of course did not know that it was Iago who had instigated Roderigo into murdering him, and then stabbed Cassio himself. As the injured man continued to cry for help, Iago pretended to be concerned and asked, 'Oh, what villains have hurt you so badly?' Cassio pointed to Roderigo, who was also lying hurt nearby, moaning in pain. Before he could open his mouth and reveal to Cassio who had really been the mastermind behind the murder, Iago stabbed him to death.

Turning back to Cassio, he made a show of concern, and

bound his wound with his own shirt. At that time, Bianca happened to be passing by. Seeing Cassio hurt so badly, she was almost moved to tears. Iago asked Cassio if he suspected anyone might have commissioned his murder. But Cassio had no idea. And soon he fainted from excessive blood loss. Bianca could no longer control her emotions and cried out Cassio's name. Iago pointed towards her in an accusatory fashion and told Gratiano and Lodovico that he believed it was Bianca's infamy that had brought about all this trouble. He turned upon Roderigo's dead body and exclaimed in surprise, 'Why, the murderer is my very own friend, Roderigo from Venice!'

Being a skilled actor, he pretended to be shocked and thoroughly puzzled by all the recent happenings. He apologised to Gratiano and Lodovico for not showing them proper respect. Then he called for a stretcher for Cassio, and at the same time consoled Bianca.

By that time Cassio had come back to his senses. Iago asked him, 'The man who tried to kill you was my friend Roderigo. How is it that he was your enemy?' The confused Cassio had no answer.

When Cassio had been carried out, Iago remarked at Bianca's pale face. Trying to put the blame on Bianca, he asked the other two gentlemen to keep a watchful eye on her, claiming, 'The guilty speak volumes, even when they say nothing.'

At that point Emilia came looking for Iago, anxious to know what had happened. Once again Iago made up a story and told her, 'Cassio was attacked here in the dark by some men, and one of them was my friend Roderigo. The others escaped, but Roderigo was left behind and died at my hands. Cassio was badly hurt and has been taken for treatment.'

He asked Emilia to find out where Cassio had been for dinner, and added that this was the fate of men who frequented whorehouses. He cast a meaningful glance towards Bianca and asked, 'Does that make you uncomfortable?'

Bianca promptly answered back, 'He did have supper at my place tonight. But that has got nothing to do with this.' Having got the confession that he was aiming for, Iago immediately asked Bianca to follow them. He asked Emilia to run to Othello and Desdemona and acquaint them with what had happened. To himself he assured that the outcome of this night would finally settle his future.

***

Othello finally returned to his bedchamber with a candle, where Desdemona was fast asleep. He had already made up his mind to kill her, but his great love for his wife made him pause. He looked at her longingly, and tried to control the great turmoil in his mind. He told himself that he had enough reasons to kill her. But once again he was awed by her beauty, and decided to kill her without leaving any scar on her flawless skin. But try as he might, he could not restrain himself any longer and stooped to kiss her in her sleep. Although overwhelmed by her beauty, his determination to punish her remained stronger.

Othello's kiss awoke Desdemona. 'Is that you, Othello?' she

said. 'Won't you come to bed, my lord?' she asked. 'Have you said your prayers tonight, Desdemona?' Othello said in reply. 'Is there still any crime that you have not asked forgiveness for? This is the time, because if I kill you before you confess your crimes, you might go to hell.' Othello's voice was ominous.

Desdemona was confused. 'I feel scared of you when you behave that way, my lord. I know I am not guilty and do not know what crime you are referring to. If I have committed any sin, it is that I have loved you too much,' she replied with a heavy heart. She was filled with terror to see Othello shaking all over, biting his lower lip as if trying to restrain himself. It still did not occur to her that he had really come to take her life.

Othello started accusing her of things she did not have the faintest idea about. 'The handkerchief I had gifted you with so much love,' he bellowed, 'you gave away to Cassio! How could you? He has also admitted that he has used you unlawfully. How did you think I would never come to know? Thank God that Iago took care of everything, including your beloved Cassio!'

Othello's rage frightened Desdemona. She tried to tell Othello the truth, but in vain. 'Bring him here. Cassio will tell you the truth,' she said.

Seeing that Othello would not relent, Desdemona pleaded with her husband to not kill her. 'Please let me live for some time more,' she cried again and again, but to no avail. Othello smothered her, for fear that if he delayed it any longer, he might lose the strength to kill her.

At this point Emilia called to him frantically, asking him to open the door. Desdemona was lying still, almost dead. Othello drew the curtains around her bed and let Emilia in. She gave him the news of the violence going on outside, of how Cassio had murdered Roderigo. Othello was crestfallen that Cassio was still alive and that his revenge had been spoiled. Suddenly Desdemona cried out, 'Oh, I have been falsely murdered, and I die an innocent woman.' Bidding farewell to Othello, she breathed her last.

Othello broke down and confessed that he had killed Desdemona. 'She had betrayed me, Emilia. She was a whore who had cheated on me with Cassio. It was your own husband, who knew of all this and had told me everything.'

Emilia was stupefied. It was hard for her to believe that Iago could have been the instigator of such violence. 'My husband, you say? My husband had told you?' Not able to restrain herself any longer, she turned towards Othello and said, 'My mistress was too fond of you, never realising what treachery was under way. Iago has lied all through, and convinced you that she had been unfaithful! You can kill me too with that sword of yours, I have no fear. But I want to tell everybody of your crime before I die.'

While Othello drew his sword, Emilia started shouting out his crime. Montano, Gratiano and Iago rushed into their chamber along with some other men. Pointing towards

Iago, Emilia cursed him and asked him to confess his crime. 'It is because of your lie that my mistress lies dead right now,' she cried. Everyone present was shocked. Emilia refused to listen to Iago anymore, who kept asking her to keep quiet and ordered her to go home. Gratiano, who was Desdemona's uncle, was greatly grieved. 'Thank God your father died out of grief. Had he been here to see you like this tonight, he would have been badly hurt,' he sighed. Othello tried without success to tell them of the reason—his belief that Desdemona and Cassio were lovers. Emilia, who knew the truth, gasped on hearing this, cursing Iago even more vehemently. Iago drew out his sword to silence Emilia. She confessed that it was Iago who had made her steal that handkerchief from Desdemona.

And finally Othello realised how he had been misled by Iago. He ran to grab him, but by then Iago had stabbed Emilia and fled. Emilia died singing Desdemona's last song.

Othello was writhing in pain and guilt. He took out a sword, hardened in ice-cold water and razor-sharp. Gratiano returned at that moment and drew back in fear that Othello might hurt him.

At this time, Lodovico and Montano entered, followed by Cassio who was being carried on a stretcher. Then came some officers with Iago under arrest. Without sparing a second thought, Othello stabbed Iago the moment he was brought forward. The others quickly took away his sword.

Slowly the truth dawned on everyone. Othello confessed

to having contrived Cassio's murder, and having killed his wife himself. He apologised sincerely to Cassio. Iago swore silence and refused to speak. Lodovico handed over two letters which they had found in Roderigo's pocket, which revealed how Iago had been instigating Roderigo to kill Cassio and falsely promising to help him win over Desdemona. Othello realised how terribly he had been manipulated. 'Oh! What a fool I am!' he cried out.

The letters also revealed how Iago had planned Cassio's demotion. Lodovico asked Othello to step down as the governor of Cyprus, after which Cassio would replace him. Othello was to be put under arrest. But it did not matter—Othello was too distraught at having killed his wife. He made an appeal to everyone to not judge him too harshly. 'Remember me as someone who did not love wisely, but loved with passion, as someone who did not easily become jealous, but fell prey to wicked suggestions.' He then took his sword, and plunged it deep into his own breast, kissing Desdemona as he died. 'I kissed you as I killed you, and now I shall die upon a last kiss from you!' were his final words.

Cassio became Governor of Cyprus, and he ensured that Iago met with a fitting punishment for his malicious deeds.

# Supplementary Reading

# Character Sketches

## OTHELLO

Othello is a brave soldier who becomes a general in the Venetian army. He is a descendant of a noble family, and fights commendably against the Turks for the Venetians. Being a Moor, he is a dark-skinned man, and much of the anger against him emerges from the prejudices against his race.

For a large part of the play, Othello is jealous and suspicious, and betrays a mad temper. While Othello loves his wife Desdemona immensely, he is never confident that she is as faithful and loving, because he is afraid Desdemona may leave him for a European man, more handsome, younger, and with fairer skin. Although Othello's characteristics are conveniently ascribed to his race by several Venetians, we must keep in mind that Othello was misled by the supremely cunning Iago, who used these race prejudices to his advantage. While it may seem that Othello is easily misled, it must also be remembered that Iago successfully deceives not only the Moor, but also several Venetians, including Roderigo, Cassio and his prostitute-friend Bianca.

## DESDEMONA

Othello's wife, and Brabantio's daughter, is the ideal noble lady—cultured, refined and beautiful. She falls in love with Othello because of the stories he tells her about his many adventures and the innumerable hardships he has endured with bravery in his life. We see more evidence of her benevolence and sympathy when she tries to help Cassio after his demotion, not knowing she is falling further and further into Iago's trap and worsening her husband's jealousy. In spite of the many accusations she is faced with, Desdemona remains an epitome of faithfulness and loyalty.

She is made of steadfast qualities, and proves that she is assertive as well, choosing to marry Othello against her father's wishes, and even though his race is suspect in the eyes of the Venetians. Desdemona is the only person in the play who does not condemn Othello based on her society's prejudices against his race.

## IAGO

The ensign of Othello, Iago is a Machiavellian man whose extreme maliciousness wreaks havoc on every major character in the play. He tends to suspect people he dislikes of having illicit relations with his wife. His displeasure against Cassio stems from what he perceives as the latter's unwarranted promotion to the position of Othello's lieutenant. His anger towards Othello is also likely for the same reason—because he chose as Lieutenant someone who Iago thinks is incompetent as opposed to himself. It is also possible that he is racially motivated against Othello. However, he understands people's strengths and weaknesses well and uses them to his advantage and for the furthering of his plans. All the major characters in the play are at his mercy.

Iago's attitude towards women is extremely problematic. He sees them only as quenchers of men's sexual needs. Other than that, woman are good for nothing, just cunning creatures who use their charms to trap men.

It is Iago's actions and motivations that decide the course of events in the play, making him one of the most significant characters in *Othello*.

# Questions

### 1

a. Who is Othello?

b. Who is Iago? Why is Iago angry with Othello?

c. Who is Roderigo? How is he used by Iago?

d. What is Brabantio's complaint to the duke?

e. How does Othello defend himself in front of the duke?

f. Why does Desdemona accompany Othello in battle?

### 2

a. How do the Venetians win the war against the Turks?

b. How does Iago poison Roderigo's mind against Casssio?

c. Who is Montano? Why does he fight with Cassio?

d. Why is Cassio demoted? How does he plan to win back his position?

e. Is Roderigo's role as the gullible lover believable?

### 3

a. Why does Othello not want to reinstate Cassio?
b. Why does Iago help Cassio in meeting Desdemona?
c. How does Iago want to make Othello jealous?
d. How does Desdemona lose her handkerchief?
e. How does Iago convince Othello of Desdemona's infidelity?

### 4

a. Who is Bianca? How does Iago use Cassio and Bianca to further Othello's suspicion?
b. Why does Cassio want a copy of the handkerchief?
c. Why does Othello shout at Desdemona?
d. How does Iago convince Roderigo to continue helping him?

### 5

a. How does Iago betray Roderigo?
b. How does Othello kill Desdemona?
c. How does Emelia die?
d. How does Othello die? What is the dying act?
e. Do you think Othello had any options other than suicide after killing Desdemona?

# *As You Like It*

William Shakespeare

**Retold by**
**Anurima Chanda**

# Characters

Duke Senior

Jaques and Amiens: *noblemen attending on Duke Senior*

Duke Frederick: *brother to Duke Senior*

Le Beau: *courtier attending on Duke Frederick*

Charles: *a wrestler*

Oliver, Jaques and Orlando: *sons to Sir Rowland de Boys*

Adam and Dennis: *servants to Oliver*

Touchstone: *a court fool*

Sir Oliver Martext: *a country vicar*

Corin and Silvius: *shepherds*

William: *a country yokel*

Rosalind: *daughter to Duke Senior*

Celia: *daughter to Duke Frederick*

Phebe: *a shepherdess*

Audrey: *a country wench*

Other lords, pages, attendants and a person representing Hymen

# 1

Sir Rowland de Boys, a well-respected wealthy man with a large estate, had three sons, Oliver, Orlando and Jaques. When he died, he left behind a large fortune, but in those days, only the oldest son could inherit the whole of his father's estate. Thus Sir Rowland's entire estate went to Oliver. On the other hand, Orlando had inherited all the noble qualities of his father, which displeased his older brother greatly. Oliver was secretly jealous of Orlando's innate goodness which made him popular among his people.

The only person who was close to Orlando was Adam, the old and loyal servant of the de Boys family. Feeling depressed about his disempowered situation, Orlando shared his anger and grief with him. 'I feel as if I have been kept like an animal in its stall. Neither am I sent to school for education, like my brother Jaques, nor am I taught the manners suited for a gentleman's son,' he said. 'Even his horses are cared for and trained better, but I, his brother, have nothing to gain from him. My birth into this noble family has come to mean nothing.'

While Orlando was complaining about his condition and telling Adam how he could no longer bear his brother's unjust treatment, which made him want to revolt against him, Oliver arrived. Seeing Orlando, he asked, 'What are you doing here?' Orlando lashed back wittily at his brother saying that he was doing nothing since he had been taught to do nothing. Oliver showed his displeasure at Orlando's ways and asked him not to waste his time. This led to another quarrel, as Orlando rebuked Oliver for he seemed to have inherited very little of the nobleness their father was known for. Orlando retorted, 'Though you are the eldest and thus entitled to inherit Father's property, do not forget that the same blood runs in my veins. At least I know how to behave with you, treat you with respect, but do you know your duties towards me?'

At this, Oliver struck Orlando, which further enraged him. Being a man of great physical strength, Orlando seized Oliver's hands. He refused to let go of him unless he promised to give Orlando the little share of their father's property that had been allotted to him. Threatened by Orlando, Oliver agreed to give him his share but on the condition that he would have to leave the estate immediately. He also insulted Adam and ordered him to leave with Orlando. Hurt and saddened by such treatment after being in their service for so long, Adam remembered his kind old master fondly, and then left along with Orlando.

Oliver was left alone to ponder over this sudden turn of events. 'Orlando has grown too big for his boots,' he thought. 'I will have to do something about it so that I can teach him a lesson without having to give him his thousand crowns.' He then called his servant Dennis and asked him to send in Charles, the duke's wrestler, who had come to meet him. While Dennis went to fetch Charles, Oliver murmured to himself, 'With the wrestling match scheduled for tomorrow, I know just how to take care of the situation at hand.'

Oliver greeted Charles as he came in. 'What is the news at the new court?' he asked. Charles had only old news to give him. 'Duke Frederick has usurped the duchy from its rightful owner, his older brother, Duke Senior. Duke Senior has taken refuge at the Forest of Arden along with a few of his loyal followers. However, the duke's daughter Rosalind has been permitted to stay at the court, being the oldest and closest friend of Duke Frederick's daughter, Celia,' he informed.

Oliver then asked him whether he was to wrestle before this new duke the next day. On hearing this, Charles confessed that he had actually come to speak to him about that very wrestling match. He had come to know secretly that Orlando was planning to participate in this match in disguise. However, this match was an important day for Charles, who wanted to prove his capabilities before the new duke. He would be ruthless at the match, sparing no pity for anybody, even Orlando. However, out of his great love for Oliver, he had come to warn him to ask his brother to withdraw from the match and prevent him from hurting Orlando.

'I thank you for your concern,' replied Oliver, 'but I have already tried my best to dissuade Orlando from fighting this match, although without any success.' Painting an evil picture of Orlando, Oliver tried to manipulate Charles. 'My brother is a stubborn and envious man,' he said. 'He does not even refrain from plotting against me, his own sibling.' Saying this, he advised Charles to injure him fatally, before Orlando tried to do the same to Charles through wrestling or by some other indirect means.

After Charles left, Oliver congratulated himself on his clever scheming and hoped that his plot would succeed in bringing an end to Orlando's life.

***

At the duke's palace, the wrestling match took place the very next day. Lots of people gathered to watch Charles overthrow every opponent who dared to challenge him. There were however two ladies who were busy talking to each other, not paying any attention to the matches. They were Rosalind and Celia. The cousins were close friends and shared everything with each other. Celia was not unaware of Rosalind's misery over her father's banishment and separation from her. She tried her best to cheer her friend up. She said, 'What is yours will be restored to you and will always remain yours! Though I am the only daughter of my father, you will be his heir after his death. I promise to return to you what my father has snatched from you.' Rosalind too was extremely fond of her cousin. For her sake, she tried to forget all her woes and engage in some tomfoolery with her. They were joined by Touchstone, who was the fool at the Duke's court and whose witty remarks were enough to keep the ladies entertained.

However, seeing them completely detached from the sport that was entertaining the whole dukedom, one of the royal courtiers, named Le Beau, came to persuade them to join the audience. While he was busy narrating to them how Charles had overthrown all the three sons of an old father, the wrestling match moved closer to where they were, and Rosalind noticed that the present suitor was a young handsome boy.

Little did she know that this was none other than Orlando, whose father had been one of Duke Senior's loyal followers. Fearing that he might be badly injured and defeated by Charles, Rosalind felt an inexplicable sense of protection towards him. Both the cousins called upon Orlando and tried to convince him of the perils that lay ahead of him and tried to make him withdraw, but Orlando was too determined to be persuaded otherwise. Realising that no amount of pleading would make him change his mind, the cousins wished him luck and let him go. However, they soon learnt that their fears were unfounded as Orlando managed to overthrow Charles as quick as lightning.

The duke was extremely impressed by his strength and vigour, but on hearing that he was the son of Rowland de Boys, an ardent supporter of Duke Senior, his entire demeanour towards Orlando changed. He said, 'I wish you were somebody else's son. Though the world revered your father, he will always remain an enemy to me.' Saying so, he ordered Orlando to leave his palace.

Rosalind, on the other hand, was more than pleased to learn of his lineage. She was gradually falling in love with this handsome, gallant man, whose father had been a favourite of her own father. Distressed at Duke Frederick's harsh behaviour towards Orlando who she thought was well deserving of nothing but compliments, Celia and Rosalind went to congratulate him. As a token of her appreciation, Rosalind presented him with a chain and bid him farewell. Orlando himself was attracted towards Rosalind and became tongue-tied in front of her. Though Rosalind kept coming back, giving him ample scope for conversation, Orlando just stood there like a lifeless block.

'I seem to have been finally overthrown by some strong passion!' lamented Orlando, seeing both of them leave. At this point, Le Beau came to advise him to leave the palace as soon as possible for his own safety. Orlando took this opportunity to ask him about the two ladies. Le Beau told him all about Rosalind and Celia and how Rosalind had been detained at the palace to keep her cousin company, since both of them loved each other more than natural sisters are capable of. He also told him how Duke Frederick had taken a sudden displeasure to his gentle niece and that it would not be long before she would meet the same fate as her father. Saying this, he departed, leaving Orlando behind to ponder over the beauty of Rosalind and the likeness of their situation.

***

Meanwhile, in another part of the palace, Rosalind and Celia were engaged in joyful banter. Rosalind complained, 'Oh how my heart aches!' Celia knew well the cause of such heartaches, and jokingly teased her. 'My dear Rosalind, it's time for you to "wrestle" with your emotions.' She made the reference to Orlando clear. Suddenly, Duke Frederick arrived, along with his lords. He ruined the cousins' playful mood with his order of Rosalind's banishment, her sole fault being that she was Duke Senior's daughter. He told Celia, 'It was only because of your sake that Rosalind had been kept back. But she is no longer a child and has cleverly gained the sympathy of the people with her subtlety and patience. For your own sake, she needs to be banished, so that the people can appreciate you more than her.'

On hearing this, Celia felt devastated. She said to her

father, 'It was your own decision to make Rosalind stay. I was too young then to know her value. But now I know what she means to me. If she is banished, I'll go with her, because I cannot live without Rosalind.' But nothing could alter Duke Frederick's decision. He left after warning Rosalind that if she did not leave within ten days, she would be put to death.

Celia was determined to leave with Rosalind. She suggested that they go in search of Duke Senior in the Forest of Arden. However, knowing that travelling so far off was dangerous for girls, they decided to disguise themselves. Rosalind being the taller of the two, would dress up like a man and go by the name of Ganymede, while Celia would become Aliena, Ganymede's sister. They also decided to convince Touchstone and take him along with them so that they would have someone who could provide them with entertainment and comfort.

# 2

Meanwhile, in the Forest of Arden, Duke Senior was leading a happy life, away from the artificialities of the court. Though they were living amidst a lot of adversity, the duke was willing to accept all his hardships, thinking them to be the penalties for Adam's fall and comparing his surroundings to those of Eden. His loyal companions who had accompanied him on his exile, were more than happy to agree with the duke. Amiens was one among them, who seemed to find sweetness in their life in the forest.

However, the duke was also aware of the fact that their stay at the forest had endangered the lives of the animals there. For their own survival, it was absolutely necessary that they kill the animals there for food. The natives of the forest seemed to have fallen prey to man's violence. One of the lords agreed with the duke, and told him about Jaques, another nobleman who had come to the forest with the duke, who had the most melancholic demeanour among them all. The lord narrated how he and Amiens had spotted him lying under an oak tree near a brook, where a lonely stag wounded by the hunter's arrow had come to languish. Jaques grieved at the condition of this stag, swearing that Duke Senior was no less a usurper than his younger brother, having taken over the rightful place of these animals, and leaving them to die pitiable deaths. He cried at the animal's pain, and was unhappy that it was being killed at its own home, abandoned by its brethren. The lords had left Jaques there, sobbing and ranting at the stag's condition. Knowing that Jaques, with his passion and melancholic disposition, would be a source of healthy debate, Duke Senior was eager to meet him, and asked the lords to take him to Jaques.

***

The news of Celia's absence had reached Duke Frederick by this time. He felt very angry and was suspicious that some of his enemies at court might have helped her and Rosalind escape. One of his lords told him that Celia's lady attendants had found them missing from their rooms in the morning, while another lord informed him of Touchstone's absence, suspecting that he might have accompanied the cousins. Hisperia, one of their attendants, confessed that she had overheard the cousins making much of Orlando, after he overthrew the notorious wrestler Charles. 'She also believes that they might have escaped with his help and in his company, said the lord.

Duke Frederick was so enraged by this news that he immediately issued orders to his people to look for Orlando at his brother's estate. He was to be fetched and brought before the duke. Failing that, Oliver was to be brought instead.

***

Meanwhile, at Oliver's estate, Adam was letting Orlando in on his brother's conspiracy against his life. Oliver had heard of Orlando's performance at the wrestling match and of the praises he had earned. He had always been jealous of the virtue and valiance Orlando was known for, which made him everyone's favourite. Now, hearing of his latest victory against Charles, Oliver had been moved to such envy that he planned to set fire to Orlando's lodging and burn his brother alive. And in case his plan failed, he had thought of other means to kill his younger brother. 'It does not matter where you go, but leave this place immediately!' Adam warned Orlando.

Orlando was at his wit's end. Neither did he have any money nor had he been trained in any skills that would help him survive on his own. 'I would rather die by my brother's malice than turn into a beggar or a thief,' he declared. And yet again, Adam came to his aid. He offered Orlando his meagre savings as well as his services, pleading with Orlando to leave the estate and take him along on his journey.

Orlando was touched by this gesture. Praising the goodness of the old, he decided to let Adam come along and look for some humble job, away from Oliver's estate. Adam pledged his loyalty towards Orlando and felt glad at having been of such help to his master. 'What an appropriate way to pay off my master's debt and die a free man!' he exclaimed.

***

In the meantime, Rosalind, Celia and Touchstone had reached the Forest of Arden, extremely weary from their long-drawn journey. Looking for shelter, they chanced upon two men, one old and the other young, engaged in solemn talk. They were two shepherds, old Corin, whose brutish master had put his pastures and flocks on sale, and young Silvius, who wanted to buy them but was caught up in a more intense passion, being in love with Phebe, a shepherdess. Rosalind overheard Silvius telling Corin of his love for Phebe, the ridiculous things he would do for this love, his fantasies and his belief that no one's love could compare to his. Rosalind was instantly reminded of her own budding love, and she found herself pining for Orlando.

Touchstone was provoked by Rosalind's lovelorn state to poke some fun at her. Rosalind was not the least offended, but jested along with him wittily. They were interrupted by Celia, almost fainting with fatigue, who asked them to find out if old Corin could provide them with some food. Touchstone and Rosalind called out to Corin, and pointing at Celia's condition, asked him where they could find some food and shelter.

'I pity her condition and would really like to help you all,' said Corin, 'but I myself am dependent on my master and do not own anything of my own. Moreover, my master, who is an uncaring man, has put his property on sale and is no longer here. Thus, I have nothing I could offer except for the bare little I have, which you are welcome to use.' He also told them that Silvius was to buy the flock and pastures, but being in a state made poor by love, he couldn't afford to buy very much.

Since Celia had already fallen in love with the place, Rosalind told Corin they would be willing to buy the property and also work for them, but only if in doing so they would not be wronging Silvius. Corin gladly accepted their offer and helped them purchase the property and settle down on that fertile tract of land.

***

In another part of the forest, Amiens was singing a song celebrating the beauty and goodness of the pastoral in all its roughness. Jaques sat listening to him, begging for more each time he stopped. Amiens indulged him and promised to sing him the rest of the song. But before he continued, he asked the rest of the lords to lay the banquet table for the duke, who had been on the lookout for Jaques since morning. Jaques confessed that he had been avoiding the duke since morning, being tired of his argumentative nature. Then he asked Amiens once again to finish his song.

*'If ambition you have none,*
*And you love to live in the sun,*
*You hunt for your food,*
*And all you get is good,*
*Come here and see,*
*There's no enemy,*
*Only winter and rough weather.'*

To this, Jaques added a verse of his own, and asked Amiens to sing it in the same tune. But melancholic Jaques, coloured the lines with bitterness, calling all of them fools to have left their wealth and ease of life and come to suffer so. After making his cynical contribution, Jaques expressed his desire to take a nap, leaving Amiens to go and usher the duke to his newly set banquet.

***

Meanwhile, Orlando and Adam also happened to reach the Forest of Arden. Completely fatigued after their wearisome journey, Adam confessed to Orlando that he no longer had the energy to move any further. 'I feel I might die without food. Farewell, kind master,' he cried.

Encouraging him to hold out a little longer, Orlando tried to cheer him up. He asked Adam not to give up so soon. 'I will go looking for food,' he said. 'So I command you to stay alive till I am back. Even if this forest yields something savage, I will either be food for it, or bring it as food for you. If you die before I am back, I will take it to mean that you do not appreciate my labour.' Saying this, Orlando went to look for food, leaving Adam in better spirits.

***

Duke Senior was busy looking for Jaques at his banquet, wishing to speak to him, when he suddenly emerged looking merry, which was unlike his usual demeanour. 'I have met a courtly fool in a motley coat, that too in this forlorn forest!' he exclaimed. 'He sat there railing at Lady Fortune, and when I greeted him, addressing him as "fool" he promptly replied, saying he should not be called that till heaven had sent him some fortune. Then in his fool-like manner, he ranted against the passage of time and how man rots with each passing hour.' Hearing the fool speak so wisely, meditating aloud on the ravages of time, Jaques felt enthralled, and wished to be like the fool himself. He had not been able to stop laughing ever since this encounter.

'What fool is this?' the duke asked. Jaques replied, 'He was a worthy fool! He says he had been a courtier and his brain seemed to be crammed with innumerable observations which found outlet through his wit in jumbled forms.' He also asked for a motley coat from the duke, a wish the duke agreed to grant.

Jaques was happy, and said that it was the only thing that he desired. He would then no longer remain the wise man who philosophised on everything anymore. Being wise was for him a rotten idea. 'If I am the fool, I will have freedom to lambast anyone I please. Even though people are irritated by my jokes, they will have to laugh out loud. This is the advantage of being the professional fool. For it would be considered stupid to feel offended by a fool's criticism, so nobody would dare show offence. And even if they did, the fool could just befool them again by telling them that the joke was actually on somebody else.'

Foreseeing an opportunity for provoking further debate, the duke remarked, 'I can very well predict what you would do. You would take this opportunity to chide everybody else for sinning. This is because you yourself have engaged in such lustful sins that you want to cleanse yourself by placing the blame on others.' Jaques countered this argument by stating that his criticisms would not be directed at anyone in particular but be more generally directed. 'All the situations that need to be criticised are great in number. When I berate the extreme vanity of a woman's dressing, how can I be referring to only one, when all of them are the same? Even if someone argues that his lavish clothes are none of my concern, he ends up agreeing with my criticism and thus proving that what I say is true!' At that moment he noticed Orlando, who had come looking for food with his sword drawn.

'Stop, and eat no more!' he ordered. The duke was surprised to see a respectable-looking man behave in such an unruly manner, and asked him, 'Is it your hardship that compels you to behave in such uncivil fashion or is it because you hate good manners?' Orlando replied, 'It is indeed my distress that is making me behave this way. But unless I have fed the needy, I forbid you from even touching the food that has been laid out at this banquet.'

Orlando was, however, surprised to witness such gentlemanly behaviour in such a savage forest, and soon gave up his despotic approach, and apologised for his behaviour. The duke accepted his apologies and offered him food from his table. Orlando was relieved at this invitation, but refused to be fed unless he had fed Adam. He informed the duke of the old and hungry man lying in wait for food, and at the duke's approval went out to look for Adam.

The duke was moved by this sudden turn of events. Turning to Jaques, he pointed out how life was like a theatre stage, which had in store many other sad plays apart from their own. Jaques, ready with his counter remarks, promptly answered back, 'The world is a stage, where all of us are mere actors, all of us who have their exits and entrances. Each of us has many parts to play, our lives separated into seven Acts. In the first Act we are infants, whimpering in our nurses' arms. Then we whine through our schoolboy days, with a bag of books, our bright, young faces, creeping like snails unwillingly to school. Then it's our turn to be lovers, huffing and puffing, as we write sad poems about our mistress's eyebrows. In the fourth Act, we are soldiers, ready with curses, with beards like those panthers have, eager to defend our honour and quick to fight. On the battlefield, we put ourselves in front of the cannon's mouth, risking our lives to seek fame. In the fifth Act, we are judges, with bellies fat from all the bribes we've taken. Our eyes are stern, our beards look respectable. We utter wise sayings. In the sixth Act, the curtain rises on a frail, aged man in slippers, glasses on his nose and a money bag at his side. The stockings he wore in his younger days are loose around his wrinkled legs now, and his booming voice is now merely a childish squeak. In the play's last scene—at the end of this queer, eventful history—our hero, weakened by forgetfulness, enters childhood for the second time: without teeth, without eyes, without taste, without anything.'

As Jaques reached the end of his eloquent speech, Orlando entered, carrying Adam on his back. The duke invited them to eat the food and requested Amiens to entertain them and help them to feel refreshed by singing songs and playing some music. Over food and music the duke learned that Orlando was the son of Rowland de Boys, whom the duke loved dearly. He invited both Orlando and Adam to lodge with him and the other lords, and asked them to tell him the story of their banishment.

# 3

In the meantime, Duke Frederick's orders were carried out and Oliver was brought before him at his duchy. 'It can't be true that you haven't seen your brother!' the duke bellowed. 'If you do not want to be punished yourself, find out within the next one year wherever your brother is and bring him here dead or alive, so that he may testify and absolve you of all your guilt. Till then all your land and property will be mine, and if you fail to perform your task, they will permanently become mine and you will be thrown out of your own land.'

Even though Oliver tried to convince Duke Frederick over and over again that he had never loved his brother in his life, the duke was unmoved. He called Oliver a villain and asked his men to seize his land and property and send him packing.

***

Having found shelter with Duke Senior at the Forest of Arden, Orlando was now relieved of all his worries, except for one—his blossoming love for Rosalind. Finding the forest to be a suitable place for expressing his pent-up passion, he went around carving love poems on the barks of trees, eulogising Rosalind's beauty and virtue.

While he was thus engaged, Corin and Touchstone went for a walk, pondering over the merits and demerits of a shepherd's life. Touchstone weighed everything against his former courtly life and pointed out that both worlds had its positives and negatives. Corin's observations on the other hand were simple and matter-of-fact. For him sickness was bad, while money, employment and contentment were good. He knew that it is the rain that wets and the fire which burns, the green pasture that makes sheep fat and the absence of sun that makes night. Touchstone found in him the makings of a natural philosopher; his only basis for damnation being that Corin had never been to a court. 'Because the court teaches you good manners, the lack of which breeds wickedness, which itself is a sin. And if you sin, you are damned,' reasoned the witty man.

Corin was quick to point out that what was good at the court might not necessarily be considered good in the country.

'Like the courtly way of salutation by kissing one's hand. Who would like to kiss a shepherd's greasy hand in greeting?' Corin said.

'Why? A man's hand might be greased from his sweat!' Touchstone retorted.

'But we have the hard hands of workers,' Corin argued.

'The kiss will make it easier to feel them then!' said Touchstone.

'But our hands are often tarred over with the surgery of our sheep, while your hands smell sweetly of civet!'

'I must call you a fool for this,' said Touchstone. 'Don't you know that civet is made from the discharge of cats? And that is much baser than your tar.'

Unable to compete with Touchstone's courtly wit any further, Corin gave up, much to Touchstone's annoyance. Before he could embark on another volley of witty repartee, Corin was more than happy to see his new master Ganymede (who was actually Rosalind in disguise) approaching.

Rosalind, in the meantime, had spotted Orlando's verses on several tree barks. As she read them aloud, Touchstone overheard the lines, and came to the conclusion that they were rotten rhymes which he could easily outdo with his brilliant poetic skills. But before more could be said on the subject, Celia appeared as Aliena, reading aloud a verse she had found. Seeing Touchstone and Corin, she gently asked them to leave so that she could debate the source of these verses with her cousin.

Both of them agreed that the verses were either overburdened with rhyme or too weak to be called poetry. 'But did it never occur to you what your name was doing in all these verses? Do you know who wrote them?' questioned

Celia. 'Was it a man?' asked Rosalind. Teasing her cousin, Celia remarked, 'One who has a chain hanging around his neck, a chain which belonged to you once!' Rosalind blushed in anticipation, and the more she begged Celia to tell her who it was, the more Celia pulled her cousin's leg and refrained from divulging the name. When Celia finally told her that it was Orlando, Rosalind was overjoyed and asked her questions incessantly.

Celia then told her how she had found Orlando sleeping beneath a tree, stretched out like a wounded knight, dressed like a hunter. At that very moment, both Orlando and Jaques also happened to arrive at the scene. Rosalind and Celia quickly hid themselves to keep an eye on them. Orlando and Jaques, both tired of each other's company, engaged in a witty exchange on the topic of Rosalind and love. Not willing to spend any more time with Orlando, Jaques left to look for Touchstone, whom he had chanced upon earlier. Rosalind took this opportunity to reveal herself as Ganymede before Orlando, using her disguise to her advantage. She played the part of an insolent boy, brother to Aliena, while her real aim was to torment the lovelorn Orlando in a playful manner.

'What's the time, forester?' she asked. 'But there's no clock here in the forest,' replied Orlando. 'Neither will be here any lovers then,' Rosalind said. 'Because any lover is as good as a clock, acutely aware of every minute and hour.

They spend their time in separation from their partners, sighing every minute and groaning every hour.'

Rosalind then presented an analysis of how time was different for different people, in an attempt to impress Orlando. Orlando was bemused to find such a pretty young lad speaking such refined language in an otherwise uncouth forest. Rosalind cooked up a story about a religious uncle of hers from the city, who had taught her to speak in such fashion. 'This uncle of mine had fallen in love while at the city, and constantly lectured me against it when he was back,' she said, steering the discussion to the topic of love and courtship. Taking extra precaution so that Orlando would not be suspicious, she said, 'Thank God I am not a woman myself! Or else I would have been plagued with all the offences that my uncle had heaped upon womankind itself. You want to know what evil plagues them? Such golden words of wisdom are only for the sick, for those who fall in love with women. Like this poet, who has been carving out verses about some Rosalind on every tree bark—only a good advisor can cure his disease.'

Orlando, lovesick and desperate to find this cure, was tormented further by Rosalind, who said that he did not have any of the symptoms that a man in love usually has. 'Neither a thin face nor a sleepless sunken eye, no irritable temper or a neglected beard—but then you do not seem to have much of a beard either. I can't see your stockings falling down around your ankles. Why is your hat not flying off your head? Your sleeves are not unbuttoned, your shoes aren't untied. Nothing about you demonstrates carelessness and misery. You're so neat and so carefully dressed that you look like you love yourself more than anyone else,' teased Rosalind.

Desperate to prove how much he loved Rosalind, Orlando kept slipping further and further into Rosalind's trap. Rosalind asked Orlando to imagine Ganymede to be the one he was in love with and try to woo him. 'Playing my part as your love, I will act effeminate, switch moods, be unpredictable and dreamy, full of tears one moment and all smiles the next, be passionate about everything, then abhor everything around me immediately after. I will pretend to long for you, but be proud and aloof at the same time. Most boys and women act just like this. And so will I act too. I will like you one minute and despise you the very next; cry for you, then spit on you; until finally I have driven love out of you to be replaced with anger,' finished Rosalind.

Agreeing to play along, Orlando gave in to this plan and left with Ganymede and Aliena to see where they lived, so that he could meet the criterion that had been set in order to get his cure. He decided to go to their cottage every day to woo Ganymede who would pretend to be Rosalind. Little did he know that Ganymede was Rosalind herself!

***

While Orlando set off with his new friends, Touchstone fell in love with Audrey, a country wench. Their hilarious love affair slowly unfolded, as Touchstone fruitlessly tried to woo her using the language of the court, which left Audrey untouched. Jaques, following them unseen, was amused by the situation. Touchstone finally proposed marriage to Audrey, informing her that he had already spoken to Sir Oliver Martext, the vicar from the next village, and that he had promised to meet them there and marry them, lecturing her on the subject of marriages, loyalty and the debatable character of a wife.

At this point, the vicar arrived. 'Is there no one to give the woman away in marriage?' he asked. Having no one else around, Jaques felt compelled to offer them his help. But Touchstone stopped him even before the proceedings could start. Irritated with his haste and ignorance, Jaques counselled him on the kind of marriage befitting a man of his breeding.

***

Rosalind on the other hand was almost in tears. Orlando, who had promised to come and visit her that morning, had still not arrived. Celia was a patient listener. To help her cousin overcome her feelings for Orlando, she said, 'Maybe he is no longer in love with you.' She said that she knew he was staying with her father, Duke Senior. Rosalind told Celia how he had met him and managed to fool her own father in the guise of Ganymede. But returning to the subject of love, Celia said, 'He is surely a brave man, to have professed his love so bravely and to have fallen out of it bravely enough the very next day. Why do you care about such foolish men who do not think twice before breaking your heart?'

Interrupting their discussion, Corin entered, and invited the cousins to witness a love squabble between Silvius and his lady love, the disdainful Phebe.

***

All of them crept unseen to watch Silvius, grown pale in anguish over his unrequited love, entreating Phebe to refuse his love if she pleased, but to do so lovingly. Phebe, irritated with Silvius' persistence, wished that she could kill with her eyes alone and be saved from such tortuous imploring. 'You'll know my pain only if you fall in love yourself, dear Phebe,' cried Silvius.

At this point, Rosalind, pretending to be Ganymede, addressed Phebe, puncturing her pride with harsh words. She told her how ugly she was, and rebuked Silvius for being in love with her. She asked Phebe to be thankful that she had such a nice man fall in love with her and accept whatever came her way, because ugly as she was, Silvius might be the only man that she could ever have.

Ironically enough, Phebe immediately felt attracted to Rosalind, mistaking him for a man. Rosalind realised this and warned her, 'I pray, do not fall in love with me. I am more false than the promises made by a drunkard. Moreover, know that I do not remotely fancy you! Rather, accept what you have got because you do not have beauty enough to feel the pride that you use to scorn Silvius.' Saying this, she left with Celia and Corin to tend to their sheep.

Now Phebe grew desperate to find out who that young man was who had just spoken to her so daringly. Exploiting Silvius' love for her, she coaxed him into giving her the information she wanted, and learnt about Rosalind, thinking her to be Ganymede. She finally decided to send Ganymede a taunting letter, which was to be delivered to him by Silvius.

# 4

Soon after, Jaques happened to meet Rosalind and Celia in their respective guises of Ganymede and Aliena. Thinking Rosalind to be a young lad, he ran after her, praying, 'Let me be better acquainted with you, pretty sir.' But Rosalind was in no mood to oblige Jaques. Rebuking his excessive melancholy, she tagged him as a still post, who deserved to be a subject of ridicule. Justifying his melancholic nature, Jaques said, 'My melancholia is far different from that of the insecure scholar or the temperamental musician, the proud courtier or the diplomatic lawyer, the nicety of a lady or the lover's moody disposition. My melancholy is my very own, born out of my extensive travels that keep me thoughtfully occupied at all times.'

Mocking him, Rosalind said that she would rather have a fool to make her happy than gain such experience and be eternally sad. 'And imagine, to also go through all the trouble of travelling to gain nothing but sadness!' she added.

At that moment, Orlando arrived. Greeting Rosalind,

whom he believed to be Ganymede, who was supposed to be playing the part of his beloved, that is Rosalind herself, he said, 'Good day, dear Rosalind!' This happy salutation irked Jaques, who immediately took his leave. Turning towards Orlando, Rosalind (dressed as Ganymede), pretended to play herself, giving herself airs considered very feminine, so that her true emotions would not show. She answered, 'Where have you been all this while? Call yourself a lover? Never again should you bother me with such grave lies!' Orlando asked for forgiveness and pointed out that he was only an hour late. At this, Rosalind scolded him, saying that a lover, who can bear to be apart from his lady love even for a minute, cannot really be in love.

They played along in this way, Orlando pleading with his Ganymede-Rosalind, while Rosalind kept refusing his persuasions on the pretext of teaching him the whimsical nature of all women. Celia, whom Orlando believed to be Aliena, played her part too by reminding Rosalind that she was only a man competing with the real beauty, Orlando's Rosalind.

Enjoying herself thoroughly, Rosalind provoked Orlando to woo her, asking him to imagine that she was Rosalind. Their role-play reached such heights that Aliena was called upon to be the priest and marry off Orlando to his Ganymede-Rosalind. Tormenting him further, Rosalind went on to narrate how girls change after marriage. 'They grow jealous and possessive about their man. They become noisy and demanding. They weep or laugh without reason. The wiser they are the wilder they get,' said Rosalind.

Suddenly Orlando remembered that he would have to join the duke for lunch. He asked for leave and promised to return to Ganymede at two o'clock. But Rosalind, who was enjoying the situation very much, was reluctant to let him go. Finally she agreed on one condition. 'Promise me that you will be back in exactly two hours. If you are late even by a minute, I will consider you to be the most pathetic lover, unworthy of Rosalind.' Vowing to keep this promise, Orlando took his leave.

Alone with her cousin, Celia chided Rosalind for having painted such a derogatory picture of womankind. She accused her male garb and said, 'Look how the bird has defiled her own nest!' She was so annoyed with her that she refused to even listen to her justifications, and went to sleep instead.

***

Meanwhile, the lords had settled with a hunt, and a grand party was under way. One of the lords had hunted a deer. Jaques, excited with the kill, urged the lord to present it to the duke in the manner of a Roman conqueror. One of the other lords broke into song. The entourage got ready to present their kill in front of the duke.

***

It was already past two. Rosalind was waiting for Orlando but there was still no sign of him. 'He must have gone off to sleep, with his pure love and a troubled brain,' scorned Celia. Her tirade was however cut short by Silvius' arrival. Silvius had been sent by Phebe to deliver her letter to Ganymede. The poor lover had no idea about the contents of the letter, but had assumed, judging by Phebe's sternness, that it might bear an angry message.

He did not know how he had been rendered a vehicle of Phebe's love for Ganymede, by his lady love herself. Rosalind read the letter, fuming with anger at the harsh words Phebe had used. She accused Silvius, blaming him for having a hand in the writing of the letter. 'Love has turned you into an unthinking puppet,' she said. Then she read the letter aloud.

*Are you god to shepherd turned,*
*That a maiden's heart has burned?*
*Can a woman rail thus?*
*Why, your godhead laid apart,*
*Warr'st you with a woman's heart?*
*Did you ever hear such railing?*
*Whiles the eye of man did woo me,*
*That could do no vengeance to me.*
*If the scorn of your bright eyne*
*Have power to raise such love in mine,*
*Alas, in me what strange effect*

*Would they work in mild aspect?*
*Whiles you chid me, I did love.*
*How then might your prayers move?*
*He that brings this love to you*
*Little knows this love in me,*
*And by him seal up your mind*
*Whether that your youth and kind*
*Will the faithful offer take*
*Of me, and all that I can make,*
*Or else by him my love deny,*
*And then I'll study how to die.*

Silvius was surprised to hear Rosalind call these loving words cruel. All that he had always wanted was for Phebe to address him in that way. But Rosalind had no care for Phebe's entreaties.

Realising what her cousin was up to, Celia sympathised with the poor shepherd Silvius. Rosalind was only trying to make him realise that Phebe was just using him. She told him, 'Since she has turned you into a tame animal, go and tell her if she loves me, she should love you too. And if she still refuses, I will never take her for my own. Now off you go, for I see more company approaching!'

The man who came was none other than Oliver de Boys. He had come looking for Ganymede and Aliena, carrying Orlando's handkerchief, reddened with his blood. He narrated his story. He had been lying asleep under an oak tree, wretched and homeless with overgrown hair and beard. A snake had coiled itself around him and would have surely killed him had Orlando not reached the spot. On seeing Orlando, the snake had slid into a bush, in which lay a hungry mother-lioness, waiting to pounce on Oliver. Realising it was his own brother, Orlando had fought the lioness, despite his hatred for his sibling.

He had been taken to the duke who had welcomed him and given him food and clothes. However, the lioness had torn off some flesh from Orlando's arm during their struggle. His blood loss had made him faint. Hence he had been unable to keep his promise to meet Ganymede. Oliver also confessed that he had been inhuman till then, plotting to kill his own brother. So now he sought to make amends. He had come on behalf of Orlando to tell them of all that had transpired.

Unable to stay composed any longer, Rosalind fainted. Surprised that a man should faint, Oliver rebuked her. 'You seem to lack a man's heart!' Realising her folly, Rosalind immediately told Oliver that she was just playing her part as a woman and asked him to carry back the news to Orlando as to how well she had pretended to faint like one.

# 5

Touchstone was busy convincing Audrey that they would surely get married soon. They ran into the country bumpkin William, who also loved Audrey. Touchstone, true to his nature, hurled witty repartee at him and told him that he should abandon hopes of reuniting with her. Or else he would curb his freedom, poison him, beat him with a club or stab him with a sword, or worse still, injure him with his wit.

Threatened by Touchstone's words, William quickly bid them farewell and left. Corin appeared and asked them to follow, saying their masters were looking for them.

***

Meanwhile, more drama had unfolded in another part of the forest. Oliver had taken a liking to Aliena, she had returned the love, and both of them were planning to get married. Orlando was astonished at such a quick turn of events and asked his brother, 'Do you really want to marry her?'

Besotted with Aliena, Oliver was already contemplating handing over his entire estate to Orlando so that he could settle down in the forest with his new lover, leading the life of a shepherd. Overjoyed at his brother's intensely passionate emotions, Orlando promptly gave his consent to their match, planning to get them married the very next day. He also wanted to invite the duke and all his lords to the wedding. While this talk was still on, Rosalind, still disguised as Ganymede, arrived.

'Hello, brother-in-law,' she said to Oliver.

Then turning towards Orlando, she asked him about his wound. 'Indeed I am wounded. Except that it is not by the claws of a lioness but the eyes of a lady,' Orlando replied, in an attempt to flatter Ganymede-Rosalind. Exclaiming at the wondrous news of Aliena's imminent wedding, Rosalind said, 'Their love story seems like Ceaser's brag of "I came, I saw, I conquered." It has not been a day since they met, and they are already talking of getting married!'

Orlando replied, 'As happy as I am of their coming together, I wish I too had my beloved with me. No Ganymede, I can't keep up pretences anymore. I want my real Rosalind.' At this Rosalind grew sombre and said, 'Then I will no longer tire you with my role-playing. I know that you are a gentleman, and if you really love Rosalind as much as you say you do, you will marry her tomorrow, when your brother marries my sister. I have known a magician since I was three years old, and have learnt the most powerful magic from him. Using my magical skills I will make her appear before you tomorrow.' Ganymede asked Orlando to dress in his best clothes the next day—the day he would be united with his love.

At this juncture, Phebe arrived with Silvius and said, 'It was rude of you, dear sir, to show my letter to Silvius.' Rosalind rebuked her, saying, 'I do not care for you. Why don't you love this shepherd instead, who seems to worship you?' Hurt by this rejection, Phebe asked Silvius to tell them what it meant to be in love. All of them joined in a tirade on love, at the end of which Rosalind was completely frustrated. 'Stop!' she said. She promised each of them that their wishes would be answered if they came to the wedding the next day. With this assurance, all of them dispersed and went their ways.

***

Touchstone and Audrey had also given themselves up to the celebratory mood that prevailed in the forest. They too decided to get married with everyone else. They were in the middle of making plans for their wedding, when two of Duke Senior's page boys joined them in their celebrations, and all of them broke into a happy song.

***

Finally, the much awaited day arrived. Everybody wondered whether all that Ganymede had promised would be fulfilled. Rosalind, still in disguise, joined them and said, 'If the duke keeps his word and gives his daughter to Orlando and Orlando is ready to take her as his own, if Phebe agrees to marry me and I refuse, which should lead to her being wedded to Silvius, and if Silvius agrees to this arrangement, then I too will keep my word and set these matters straight.'

After Ganymede and Aliena had left, the duke and Orlando sat there, pondering over the close likeness of Ganymede to Rosalind and how much he reminded them of her. Around this time, Touchstone arrived with Audrey and greeted them all. Both Jaques and Touchstone entered into a lively witty debate over marriage and wooing, and entertained the duke very much.

They were cut short by the appearance of Hymen, the god of marriage, followed by Rosalind, no longer in disguise, and Celia as herself as well. Hymen sang a song on marriage while all the couples were united. Amidst all this festivity, the middle de Boys son, Jaques, arrived with the news of Duke Frederick's change of heart. 'Having received news that all his enemies had taken refuge in the Forest of Arden, he had raised a large army to invade it and fight his brother. But just at the edge of the forest, he met an old religious man who spoke to him and brought about in his heart a great change. He decided to not only abandon his vengeful pursuit of his brother but even to retreat from the corrupt world. He is giving his throne to his banished brother and restoring all the men he had exiled to their rightful lands,' informed Jaques de Boys. Everyone joined in celebrations as justice and peace were restored.

# Supplementary Reading

# Character Sketches

## TOUCHSTONE

The character of the Shakespearean fool is very similar to that of the actual court fools of the Elizabethan period. Though the main job of the fool is to keep his masters entertained, he does so by using his wits to outdo other people, especially those from higher echelons of society. The advantage of being a fool can be summed up through what Jaques says about the fool being at liberty to make fun of anybody and everybody. But the person who is being ridiculed can neither show offence nor press charges against him. He has to laugh along with the fool, even if the fun is being made at his expense.

This is also what Touchstone's role is in the play. He is a fool at Duke Frederick's court. He finally accompanies Rosalind and Celia when they leave the palace to go in search of Duke Senior in the Forest of Arden. He provides comic relief on stage. Using him as a mouthpiece, the playwright criticises various institutions without having to be afraid of censorship. He is insightful about human nature, and through his wit, adds humour to his clever observations. He has a way with words, which provides a larger scope for entertainment to the audience.

He is named after the 'touchstone', which has the ability to judge the purity of precious metals. Similarly, it is Touchstone's nature to use his witty, sarcastic words to judge other characters and reveal how pure or mixed they are. He is cynical, but has the ability to laugh at himself as well as at others. His observations, combined with his characteristic wit and humour, provide a mixture of honest perspective as well as hearty laughter on stage.

## JAQUES

Jaques is the complete opposite of Touchstone. He plays a melancholic figure in *As You Like It.* Though both of them philosophise on life to a large extent, Touchstone does it with wit and humour, while Jaques is eternally immersed in melancholia and cynicism. Shakespeare creates an exaggerated representative of the intellectual man through the character of Jaques. He is well-read and well-travelled, and it is his immense stock of experience that has wiped away every trace of humour from his life. It is Jaques who is Shakespeare's mouthpiece for these famous lines: 'All the world's a stage …'

Characters like Jaques were present at the Elizabethan court to incite thought-provoking ideas in their masters' minds and provide ample scope for debate. In the absence of other means of entertainment, these discussions offered scope for healthy mental engagement. Within the scope of the play, the exaggerated pessimism of Jaques provides a kind of balance to the overtly amusing and witty atmosphere of the play.

Jaques is one of the loyal ex-courtiers who accompany Duke Senior on his exile in the Forest of Arden. He is a moody cynic, who constantly elaborates on the pessimistic side of life and speaks at length using highly poetic language.

## ROSALIND

Rosalind is the daughter of the banished Duke Senior, and Celia's cousin. She dominates the action in the play. She falls in love with Orlando and gets married to him at the end of the play. She is a wonderful mix of kindness and spirited buoyancy. She is the epitome of womanly beauty and compassion, but she also betrays a tomboyish streak, enjoying mischief and pranks as much as any other man. Her character sees the coming together of wit and beauty, courage and vulnerability, man and woman, all at the same time. This is because Rosalind dons a male disguise and takes up the name of Ganymede, when she leaves with Celia and Touchstone for the Forest of Arden in search of her banished father. She introduces a lot of the comic element in the play with her cross-dressing, the confusion regarding her multiple levels of role-playing and her wit.

There is endless comic appeal in Rosalind's lampooning the conventions of both male and female behaviour. Her character must also have aroused great anxiety and threat among Elizabethan audiences over the fact that a woman had crossed over to a man's territory, because it was strongly believed that harmony lay in both men and women carrying out their assigned roles rather than make such cross-overs. One cannot miss the strength of Rosalind's character. She is indeed one of the strongest among Shakespeare's women characters, with wit and guts that could match up to (or even go beyond) many of his male characters.

Given the time when the play was written, Rosalind's character stands apart from other female characters of that age. She not only has the courage to venture forth alone by literally 'wearing the pants' within her unit of three, but also has the wit to compete against the wit of any other. She is not even scared to criticise that which she does not approve of. She also gives her love direction through her own able hands, and is extremely vocal about her emotions, which was a rarity in the female characters of those times. She can also be tagged as a feminist because of her ability to subvert societal limitations imposed on women, and emerges as one of the strongest characters in the play and in Shakespeare's oeuvre.

# Questions

## 1

a. Who is Orlando? Why is he so upset with life? Whom does he share his grief with?
b. How and why does Oliver scheme against Orlando?
c. Who is Charles? What news does he bring with him about the new court?
d. Who are Rosalind and Celia? Describe their relationship.
e. How do Orlando and Rosalind meet and what is the consequence?
f. What order is given to Rosalind by Duke Frederick? How do Rosalind and Celia react to his order? How do they decide to carry out their plan?

## 2

a. Where has Duke Senior taken refuge after being exiled? Who all have accompanied him? What is his attitude and reaction towards their exiled state?
b. Who is Jaques? Does he agree with the duke's views? Give reasons.
c. What news of caution does Adam bring to Orlando? What do they decide to do?

d. Whom do Rosalind and her companions meet after they reach their destination? How does he help them settle down?
e. Why does the otherwise melancholic Jaques suddenly appear in high spirits? How does that inspire him to change his temperament and profession?
f. How does Orlando meet Duke Senior and his entourage? How does the duke help him out?
g. How is Jaques moved to philosophising at this point?

**3**

a. How does Duke Frederick react to Rosalind and Celia's elopement along with Touchstone? What orders does he issue as a result of this?
b. How does Rosalind come to know that even Orlando has taken refuge at the forest? How does she meet him?
c. Why does Orlando not recognise Rosalind and Celia? How does Rosalind take advantage of this?
d. Who is Audrey? How does Touchstone woo her? After he decides to tie the knot with her, whom does he request to wed them and how does this plan materialise?
e. Why is Rosalind sad and restless? How does Celia try to console her?
f. What new twist comes about in Silvius and Phebe's love story? Explain how.

## 4

a. What happens when Orlando finally comes to meet Rosalind? How does Rosalind take their role-playing one step further?
b. Why does Orlando have to leave? What promise does he make before leaving? How does Celia react to all this?
c. What does Phebe send Rosalind? How does she react to it? What message does she send back to her?
d. Who brings Rosalind the reason for Orlando's inability to keep his promise? What is the reason?
e. How does Rosalind react? What reasons does she give for such a reaction?

## 5

a. What is the news that Oliver gives Orlando? How does he react?
b. Why does Orlando feel miserable, despite his happiness at Oliver's news? What does he tell Rosalind after this? How does Rosalind respond?
c. What promise does Rosalind make to Silvius, Phebe and Orlando?
d. What news does Jaques de Boys bring? How is everything resolved at the end?

# *The Tempest*

William Shakespeare

**Retold by**
**Teesta Guha Sarkar**

## *Characters*

Prospero: *the rightful Duke of Milan*

Antonio: *his brother, the usurping Duke of Milan*

Alonso: *King of Naples*

Sebastian: *his brother*

Miranda: *daughter to Prospero*

Caliban: *slave to Prospero*

Ferdinand: *son to Alonso*

Gonzalo: *a councillor*

Adrian and Francisco: *lords*

Trinculo: *a jester*

Stephano: *a drunken butler*

Master: *of a ship*

Boatswain

Mariners

Ariel: *an airy spirit*

Iris<br>Ceres<br>Juno<br>Nymphs<br>Reapers } *spirits*

# 1

The ill-fated ship was out at sea. It had on board some of the most august personages from Italy—King Alonso of Naples, Sebastian his brother, Ferdinand his son, and Antonio the Duke of Milan.

The wedding had gone well, and the king's daughter Claribel was now Queen of Tunis. Alonso quietly mourned her departure from his life, as they sailed on the Mediterranean waters, bound for home. But soon the ship found itself amidst a frightening storm. Tempestuous noises surrounded the passengers, lightning rent the ominous sky.

'Boatswain!' the shipmaster cried. 'Speak to the mariners; tell them what needs to be done. Hurry, or the ship runs aground!'

Without wasting any time the boatswain gave instructions to the crew, shouted words of encouragement, and threw a challenge, albeit an empty one, to the obstinate storm.

Alonso and a part of his entourage had come out to the deck in order to take stock of the situation. Afraid and angry, they questioned the boatswain's expertise and hurled accusations at him.

'Where's the master, boatswain?' Antonio demanded impatiently.

The boatswain knew that the roaring waves would make no discrimination between commoner and king, but drown everyone alike. So he paid no heed to Antonio—the boatswain was not one to cower to his interfering commands.

'Return to your cabins,' he said firmly to the passengers on deck. 'You keep us from our work with your pointless talk.'

The old councillor Gonzalo warned him to not be so brusque with the king and his men. But the boatswain declared that he cared for no one more than he did for himself, and if Gonzalo could silence the elements and restore peace and calm, he would command the mariners to stop work immediately. This Gonzalo could not do, so 'Out of our way, I say,' the boatswain yelled to him and his party.

Taking note of the boatswain's complexion, Gonzalo remarked that he was certainly born to be hanged and not to die at sea. So he argued that the passengers could come to no harm if the boatswain himself would not drown.

In the meantime the storm continued to rage, making it impossible for the mariners to control the ship. Cries of frustration could be heard from the cabins, and once again Antonio appeared, this time accompanied by an angry Sebastian.

'Merciless dog, may you be wracked by disease!' Sebastian

said. Antonio joined in, 'Go hang yourself, you lazy noise-maker!' They were certain that the boatswain's efforts would come to nothing.

While Gonzalo tried to placate the two men, the boatswain turned a deaf ear to their insults, and instructed his mariners to drive the ship out to open sea again. It had come so close to an island that it was in danger of crashing on its shore.

The mariners had lost all hope. 'To prayers, to prayers!' they cried. But the hardy boatswain would not acknowledge defeat. As he continued to struggle against the storm, Antonio suggested they all sink with the king, the boatswain's efforts having failed completely. More confused noises came from the cabins as despairing passengers bade farewell to their wife and children. But Gonzalo continued to be optimistic in the face of all the chaos. 'The wills above be done, but I would gladly die on land,' he said, as the ship battled the monstrous waves.

***

On the island at whose shore the ship would finally come to rest, the young Miranda was pleading with her father. She had seen the passengers suffer as the tempest threatened to sink the vessel, and her heart had gone out to them. 'If you are indeed capable of such powers, let the storm abate, dear father,' she said to Prospero. Thinking that every person on the ship had perished, Miranda wished she could have sunk the sea within the earth before it swallowed the ship and its helpless passengers.

But she was mistaken. 'No one has come to any harm,' Prospero told her. 'Everything I have done today has been for your benefit, my daughter, unaware as you are of your origins, and that your father was once more than just a master of a humble home on an uncharted island.'

'It is time you found out who you are, and the reason for the tempest I have brought about today,' continued Prospero. 'The wreck which moved your heart to such great compassion I have carefully arranged by the use of my magical powers. You may have heard the wretched souls cry, but I can assure you that they have lost not even a hair today.'

Surprised by Prospero's explanation, Miranda sat down to listen attentively to her father as he began to relate the story of their past.

'Do you remember a time before we came to this island?' Prospero asked. 'But how can that be—you were only three then.'

'I do remember, father,' replied Miranda. 'My memories seem like dreams and do not serve as assurance, but were there not several women once who looked after me?'

There certainly were—Prospero told her—twelve years ago, when he was Duke of Milan, and father to Miranda, the only child born to him and his virtuous wife.

'It was my brother Antonio's foul play that compelled

us to leave Milan,' Prospero explained. 'But on our way out, we received much help from those who still cared for us.'

He recounted his love for his brother, a love which Antonio had returned with nothing but treason. Immersed in the study of the liberal arts, Prospero had entrusted his brother with the management of the state, and become a stranger to his own dukedom. Seeing an opportunity for overthrowing his brother, Antonio quickly learnt how to manipulate his officials into going against Prospero.

Unaware of the treachery that was under way, Prospero neglected all worldly duties and dedicated himself to the improvement of his mind, allowing Antonio's evil nature ample time to flourish. This treacherous brother began to enjoy not only the revenue of his office but also the rewards won by means of his newfound position. Deluded by the power he had unlawfully acquired, Antonio began to think himself the rightful Duke of Milan, and his ambition grew unbounded.

He knew full well of the long-standing enmity between his brother and the King of Naples. So Antonio offered the king a handsome tribute and undue homage, in return for which he asked for Milan to be conferred upon him, and that Prospero be deported from the dukedom. So at the midnight hour on the fateful night were father and daughter pushed out of the gates of Milan by several malicious ministers appointed for the purpose.

'But why did they not destroy us?' asked Miranda.

They dared not—Prospero explained—as that would reveal their true motives to one and all; they painted their foul ends a fairer colour instead. The ministers had hurried the outcasts onto a decrepit boat that had neither tackle nor sail nor mast, and left them with nothing to do but helplessly cry to the sea and the winds. There was indeed no hope in sight, but with Miranda by his side, like a beautiful angel, Prospero had felt infused with the strength to face the difficulties that lay ahead.

But they were not completely high and dry; the noble Gonzalo had secretly furnished Prospero with food and water, garments and other amenities. The kind minister had even brought Prospero several books from his library, which he knew his master prized above his dukedom. With these provisions at hand, they travelled on foreign waters till they reached the shores of an unknown island. 'And on this island have I been your schoolmaster,' said Prospero, 'and from my lessons you have made more profit than vain princes can ever hope to from what their careless tutors can offer.'

Miranda expressed her heartfelt gratitude, but also reminded her father that she was yet to be apprised of the reason for the dreadful storm. 'There isn't time,' Prospero told her. 'Cease further questions, as an auspicious star now shines on me, and I must make the most of my fortunes immediately lest they start to droop again.'

Getting up abruptly, Prospero called for his servant Ariel to show himself. Then by his sleight of hand he caused his daughter to feel an overwhelming drowsiness. And before long, Miranda was sleeping soundly.

By this time Ariel arrived and described to his master's satisfaction how he had roused the tempest and made the waves tremble, causing shock on deck and in every cabin, exactly as Prospero had bade him do. Prospero congratulated the spirit for performing the tasks impressively, but asked if the shipwrecked passengers were safe.

'Not a hair out of place,' informed Ariel, 'not even a blemish has marred their garments. I have followed every order you gave, and dispersed the people in groups all over the island. All but Ferdinand, the king's son, who I have left by himself at a corner of the isle, where he is sitting even now, his arms folded in a sad knot.' The king's ship was safe too, hidden away in a nook, where Ariel had charmed the mariners into a deep sleep.

It was already past noon. The hours between then and six were to be used valuably. But before he resumed duties, Ariel reminded his master of the reward he had promised. 'For the constant toils I have performed at your behest, you owe me my liberty.' But Prospero did not take kindly to this demand. 'Ill-humoured servant! You make too much of the tasks you have performed. Do you forget the torment I freed you from?' he said.

Years ago, several acts of sorcery had caused Sycorax to be banished from the city of Algiers. She and Caliban, her son, had been left on this island by sailors. Sycorax had then employed Ariel to do her bidding, who was too delicate to perform the earthy tasks she would set him. He had refused, and in a fit of mad rage, Sycorax had imprisoned him in a tree. There he remained for twelve years, till Prospero came to live on the island, heard his desperate howls for help and set him free.

'If you continue to complain,' Prospero threatened, 'I will fasten you with a peg inside an oak tree and let you howl away for twelve more winters.' So Ariel begged his master's pardon and promised to be more submissive; it was only two more days till Prospero would grant him his freedom after all. Then he left to turn himself into a water nymph and become invisible to all but himself and Prospero.

It was time to pay Caliban a visit. So Prospero awoke Miranda, who said she wasn't keen on laying eyes on their hateful slave. But her father reminded her that they could not do without him either. 'He makes our fire, fetches us wood, and performs other tasks that benefit us greatly.'

Outside Caliban's cave, Ariel appeared as a nymph, in whose ear Prospero whispered further instructions. In the meantime Caliban emerged, greeting father and daughter with foul curses. 'May your bodies be covered in blisters!' he shouted.

Prospero promised to punish him severely for his surly behaviour, but no threat was powerful enough to convince Caliban that Prospero's treatment was justified. 'This island's mine by Sycorax my mother,' he said. 'You have usurped it from me.'

When they first came to the island—Caliban recalled—Prospero and Miranda had taken great care of him, fed him berries and taught him their language. Caliban had returned the favour by familiarising them with the island, showing them where the fresh springs were, leading them to the fertile areas and steering them away from the brine pits. But soon Prospero grew intolerant and confined his benefactor in a rocky cave, keeping him from the rest of the island of which he was once master.

'Lies!' Prospero yelled on hearing this. 'Only whips and not kindness can move you to humility. I have treated you with care and lodged you in my own cell, till you tried to ravish the honour of my daughter!'

'And had you not prevented me, I would have peopled this island with many little Calibans,' retorted the slave.

Enraged by this comment, Miranda burst into a diatribe against him, enumerating all the benefits he had made from their association. She accused Caliban of belonging to a vile race, which had made him ungrateful and invite punishment upon himself.

Caliban was not ready to relent either. He thanked Miranda for teaching him to speak her tongue as that had enabled him to curse as well. 'May the red plague put an end to your life for making me learn your language!' he said.

Prospero stepped in at this point, ordering Caliban to fetch them firewood and threatening to rend his body with cramps and aches if he refused. Although reluctant, Caliban was well acquainted with the power Prospero could wield, so he finally deigned to obey his order.

Meanwhile, at another part of the island, Ferdinand was still in mourning, thinking he had lost his father forever to the sea. Ariel observed him in his sad state and filled the air with an enchanting song. It seemed to calm the sea's fury; it soothed Ferdinand's mind. So charming was this song that he couldn't help but follow it till it finally came to a stop.

But before long the music could be heard again:

*Full fathom five your father lies,*
*Of his bones are coral made;*
*Those are pearls that were his eyes,*
*Nothing of him that does fade*
*But does suffer a sea-change*
*Into something rich and strange ...*

'This song is in memory of my father,' thought Ferdinand. 'There is something supernatural about its sound; I hear it now above me.' He continued to walk, hoping to find the source of this magical sound.

Ariel had led Ferdinand on to where Prospero was waiting with Miranda. He asked his daughter to open her eyes as Ferdinand walked in their direction.

Miranda gasped. 'A handsome spirit!' she said. But no, he was only human, much like themselves—her father explained—a survivor of the shipwreck, filled with grief and looking for his companions from whom he had got separated.

But he was a thing divine in Miranda's eyes; never before had she seen anyone as noble as Ferdinand. It pleased Prospero to see his daughter so enamoured of the king's son; this was his design after all.

Ferdinand too was awe-struck by Miranda's beauty, and took her to be the island's goddess, on whom he thought the musical spirits attended. 'Grant my prayer,' he said to her, 'for some instruction as to how one must conduct himself on this island. And my last question—are you human too like me?'

'I am, sir,' she replied. 'You mistake me for a wonder.'

Surprised to hear her speak his tongue, he informed Miranda that of all those who spoke this language he was the highest in rank. Believing his father to have drowned, Ferdinand thought he was now King of Naples.

'How the highest?' Prospero joined the conversation.

'What if the King of Naples heard you?'

Surprised once again, this time to hear Prospero speak of Naples, Ferdinand told him of his father's death in a shipwreck, which had also taken the lives of all his friends, the Duke of Milan and his brave son included.

'The Duke of Milan and his braver daughter would rebuke you this moment if only the time was right,' Prospero thought, annoyed by Ferdinand's reference to Antonio as the duke.

But Miranda wasn't upset in the least. What troubled her though was the ungentle way in which Prospero spoke to Ferdinand. When he expressed his desire to make her Queen of Naples, Prospero accused him of being an impostor who had come to the island to try and win it from its master. But Miranda protested, 'Nothing ill can dwell in a form so beautiful!'

Ignoring her remonstrations, Prospero proceeded to chain Ferdinand hand and foot. Ferdinand drew his sword in an attempt to resist, but Prospero wielded his magic staff and charmed him from moving.

'Have pity, father,' Miranda pleaded. But Prospero would not let his daughter and Ferdinand unite so easily. He intended to put obstacles in their path so they would find each other even more valuable than they already did.

'Silence!' he said to Miranda. 'One word more and I will rebuke you. You are a foolish girl for thinking that there are no other men like him, having only Caliban for comparison.'

This did not matter to Miranda, for she had no desire to see a better man. And imprisonment would not affect him one bit—Ferdinand said—if only he could see Miranda once a day from his cell.

'As free as the mountain winds you shall be,' Prospero whispered to the invisible Ariel, seeing that his plans were on the path to success. Then he ordered Ferdinand, with his hands in shackles, to follow him.

# 2

'Please be merry, sir,' said Gonzalo. He and the other lords had found themselves on an unknown island after the shipwreck, on which they now quibbled with one another.

It was the same island of which Prospero was master, but they knew nothing of his design—that his manoeuvre had brought them there, that not a single soul had perished in the storm. So Gonzalo made attempts at consolation. 'It is common for the masters of ships to suffer the loss that we have suffered. But as for our miraculous preservation, there is nothing as rare. And that is why, good sir, you must weigh your sorrow with your comfort.'

It was only with cynicism that Antonio and Sebastian responded to the garrulous councillor.

'Look, he's winding up the watch of his wit. Let the next auspicious hour strike, and we will hear him utter another witticism,' said Sebastian.

'Sir—' Gonzalo began.

'It has struck one. Tell,' Sebastian quipped.

'For every grief that is entertained, comes to the entertainer—'

'A dollar,' said Sebastian, cutting Gonzalo short.

'Dolour comes to him indeed,' Gonzalo remarked, punning on the cynical lord's comment. 'Therefore, my lord—'

'Oh how lavishly he uses his tongue!' Antonio complained, and Gonzalo was once again interrupted.

'Now who do you think will speak first?' Antonio asked the king's brother, and suggested they make a bet. 'Adrian or Gonzalo?'

'The old cock,' Sebastian said, referring to the old councillor.

'The cockerel,' said Antonio, meaning the young Adrian.

'And what will our wager be?' Sebastian asked.

'A laughter,' said Antonio.

It was Adrian who spoke first. 'Though this island seems deserted …'

'Ha ha ha.' Antonio had won the bet.

They now listened to the lord as he shared his thoughts. '… yet it has a tender, delicate air.' Gonzalo was in agreement. So luscious was the grass that it certainly looked like life could flourish there with ease. What was unusual though—he pointed out—was that their garments, instead of being ruined by the salty water, were dry and glossy, and looked as fresh as the time they had put them on in Africa, when the king's daughter Claribel got married to the Tunisian king.

'Not since widow Dido's time was Tunis graced by such an incomparable queen,' said Gonzalo.

'Widow Dido?' Adrian wanted to make sure. 'She was from Carthage, not Tunis,' he informed his audience.

'Tunis wasn't so different from Carthage then,' Gonzalo said, harking back to the time when Carthage was destroyed, and Tunis took its place as the commercial centre of the region.

Gonzalo and Adrian thus engaged in conversation again, gave their cynical listeners another opportunity to bandy words with them.

'Gonzalo's words are more powerful than Amphion's harp that raised the city of Thebes,' began Antonio. 'What impossible feat will he achieve next?'

'I think he will carry this island home in his pocket, like he would an apple, and gift it to his son,' said Sebastian.

'Then he will sow its kernels in the sea and produce more islands,' Antonio continued.

'But sir,' Gonzalo said to Alonso, reminding everyone of what was originally being discussed, 'do our clothes not seem as fresh as when we were at Tunis, attending your daughter's wedding?'

'You cram more words into my ears than I can bear at this time,' complained Alonso. He had not recovered even a little from the pain he suffered, thinking his son was lost to the sea, and his daughter to Tunis, a city so far removed from Italy that he feared he would never see her again.

Alonso's despair filled Lord Francisco with sympathy. He had kept out of the conversation all this while, but now felt urged to comfort the king. 'I saw your brave son push the waves down and ride on their backs,' said Francisco. 'He flung the hostile waters aside, and his bold head was always above the surges, and soon he reached the base of a wave-worn cliff. I have no doubt that he reached land shortly after.'

But no amount of consolation could change Alonso's mind. 'My son's gone,' he insisted.

'And only you are to blame for this terrible state of affairs,' said Sebastian. 'Everyone pleaded with you, your fair daughter included, to not marry her to a king in a land so distant. Now we have lost not only her, but your son too, on our journey back from his sister's wedding. Had you listened to us, this journey would not have taken place at all.'

The time of course was not right for Alonso to face these difficult truths. Full of pity for his grieving king, Gonzalo suggested that Sebastian be gentler in his criticism. 'Very well,' Sebastian finally conceded.

Having brought an end to this unpleasantness, the councillor began meditating on a new subject: how he would govern the island if he were its master. Ignoring Antonio and Sebastian's foolish remarks that quickly followed, Gonzalo declared that he would not follow custom, but on this island allow no business or sophisticated education, no employment of servants, no boundaries separating one piece of land from another, no farming and husbandry—in short, no occupation whatsoever. It would be an island of idle men and women, and yet they would remain innocent and pure, proving wrong all those who believed that idleness begets lust. There would be no sovereignty on it either.

'Still he would be its sovereign,' Sebastian pointed out on hearing this last remark.

'He seems to have forgotten that he declared himself master of the island,' Antonio said in agreement.

Alonso, still in mourning, felt disturbed by Gonzalo's ramblings. 'I request you to stop,' he told the councillor.

'And stop I will, your majesty,' said Gonzalo. 'These gentlemen needed an opportunity for laughter, and that is what I provided them. They are men of nimble lungs, and it takes little provocation to drive them to laugh at nothing.'

'We were laughing at you,' Antonio said defensively.

'Since you treat me like a person of no significance, I must be nothing to you,' said Gonzalo. 'So you may continue to laugh at nothing if you please.'

'What a blow he has given,' Antonio said sarcastically, having run out of arguments.

While the men continued to banter, Ariel arrived, playing a soporific tune. As if on cue, Gonzalo's lids grew heavy, and he fell asleep momentarily. The lords followed suit.

'I wish my eyes would shut too, and thereby put an end to my morbid thoughts,' said Alonso. And no sooner had he voiced his wish than sleep came to his eyes as well. 'We will guard your person while you rest,' Antonio promised, as he watched Alonso succumb to his sudden drowsiness. But Antonio soon revealed to his friend that he did not mean to keep his word.

'You see, Sebastian,' he said, 'they all fell together as if struck by lightning. How is it that we are not disposed to sleep? But no matter; an opportunity has presented itself, and I see a crown dropping on your head. Do you hear me?'

This suggestion took Sebastian by surprise. 'You seem to be talking in your sleep, Antonio,' he said. 'And such a strange sleep it is—to have your eyes wide open, be standing, speaking, moving, and yet so fast asleep.'

'My noble friend,' Antonio explained, 'it is not me, but your fortune that sleeps. I speak in all seriousness, and you must be serious too, for if you are, you will be three times greater than now.'

'Teach me how to be serious then,' said Sebastian. 'So far I have only been guided by hereditary sloth.'

So Antonio instructed his friend. He pointed to the sleeping Gonzalo, and suggested that when his time would be up not many people would remember him. And although he had insisted that Ferdinand had not survived the shipwreck, it was an idea as implausible as that of the councillor swimming in his sleep.

'I have no hope that the king's son is alive,' said Sebastian.

'Oh what a great hope you have,' exclaimed Antonio, 'out of this "no hope". Since you grant that Ferdinand is dead, tell me this—who is now the heir of Naples?'

'Claribel, for sure,' Sebastian replied.

Antonio disagreed. Claribel had become Queen of Tunis, she lived leagues away from civilised habitation, and could only rely on the sun for a messenger. It was true she might have a son, but until that son matured enough for his chin to grow hair, there would be no threat to Sebastian's position of heir apparent. So Antonio prodded him further. 'Do you see the good fortune that awaits you?'

Sebastian was beginning to see eye to eye. 'I remember you did supplant your brother Prospero,' he said.

'That I did,' said Antonio, 'and look how well his royal robes suit me. My brother's servants, who were once merely my friends, now obey my commands.'

'And what of your conscience?'

'What of it? A sore on my heel may compel me to put on my slippers, but there must be no conscience in my heart, for it does not move me at all.'

Antonio pointed to the King of Naples, sleeping on the earth he must necessarily return to in death. And this death they could administer—Antonio urged—using only three inches of their unfailing swords. Gonzalo would have to be done away with too; if he lived he would certainly be their greatest detractor. They didn't need to worry about the rest; being courtiers, they would eagerly bend to the wishes of the new rulers.

'You will be my example,' said Sebastian. 'As you got Milan, so shall Naples be mine. Now let us draw our swords!'

'My sword shall fall on your brother,' Antonio told him, 'and let Gonzalo die by yours.'

'Oh but can we have a word—'

But before Sebastian could finish, Ariel arrived again, still invisible to the conspirators. Prospero had foreseen the danger to the king's life, and sent the spirit to foil the plan to murder him. Ariel sang in Gonzalo's ear:

*While you here do snoring lie,*
*Open-eyed conspiracy*
*His time does take.*
*If of life you have a care,*
*Shake off slumber and beware.*
*Awake, awake!*

Gonzalo awoke with a start. 'Angels preserve the king!' he shouted. This broke Alonso's sleep too, who woke up to see Antonio and Sebastian with their swords drawn. 'Why do you two look so fearful?' he asked in dismay.

An explanation was quickly given. 'We stood here watching over your person,' Sebastian said, 'when we happened to hear bellowing sounds. We thought they might've been bulls, or lions even. Did the noises not wake you?'

'I heard nothing,' said Alonso.

So Antonio corroborated Sebastian's report. 'Oh it was a noise terrible enough to frighten a monster, to make the earth quake! There must have been a whole herd of lions.'

But Alonso was still unsure. 'Did you hear the noises too?' he asked Gonzalo.

'I did hear a humming, sir,' he said, vaguely remembering the song Ariel had sung in his ear. 'Strange sounds awoke me, although I cannot be sure what they were. But it is best we stand on our guard with our weapons drawn, or better still, leave this place altogether.'

Alonso was inclined to leave too. 'Let us move,' he said, 'and continue our search for my son.' The coucillor's persistence had revived some hope in him that his son may still be alive.

Ariel watched the scene with satisfaction, and left to tell his master that the king's murder had been prevented.

***

A storm was brewing again. The sound of thunder reached the earth, as Caliban walked laboriously with a burden of wood on his shoulders—another of Prospero's orders.

'May all the germs that the sun sucks up from marshes and swamps fall on Prospero and cover his body with disease!'

he said. Caliban knew the spirits in Prospero's service were always around. When they overheard his protests, they would throw him on sodden ground, make apes chatter at him and bite him, let snakes wind around his body and hiss him into madness. But the tasks Prospero set him were so abominable that it was difficult not to curse.

Caliban was quite habituated with punishment and pain. So when the court jester Trinculo came walking, he took him to be one of Prospero's servants, sent to torment him for being tardy in his work. 'I'll lie flat,' Caliban thought, 'and perhaps he will then miss me.'

Trinculo came talking to himself, expecting the heavy clouds to burst into rain any minute. 'The rain will surely come in thick drops,' he said, and looked for a place to hide. But he found Caliban instead.

'What have we here?' he exclaimed. 'A man or a fish? Dead or alive? What a fishlike smell he gives out! Now if I were in England, I could paint this fish to attract foolish holidayers and earn many a piece of silver. It is common knowledge that Englishmen make their fortune by displaying strange beasts, like the corpses of American natives. But alas, the country's beggars go around with their hands empty.'

While Trinculo continued to muse on the foibles of the English, the storm gained momentum. Finding no other place to hide, he crept under Caliban's gabardine after realising he was an islander, and not a creature of the sea.

'Such strange fellows a traveller must share his bed with under these miserable circumstances,' he said, and waited for the storm to subside.

Stephano, the court butler, had also found himself stranded on this unfamiliar island. He had however made the best of the situation and drunk himself merry. Bottle in hand, Stephano came along, singing what he thought was a despicable tune, and comforting himself by taking large swigs every time it struck him that the song on his lips was one he abhorred.

*The master, the swabber, the boatswain and I;*
*The gunner and his mate,*
*Loved Mall, Meg, and Marian, and Margery,*
*But none of us cared for Kate.*
*For she had a tongue with a tang,*
*Would cry to a sailor, 'Go hang!'*
*She loved not the savour of tar nor of pitch,*
*Yet a tailor might scratch her where'er she did itch.*
*Then to sea, boys, and let her go hang!*

Caliban heard Stephano's tune, and mistook him for another of Prospero's spirits. Fearing punishment, he cried, 'Do not torment me!' This startled the drunken butler. 'Do we have devils here?' he said. Spotting the half-concealed Caliban, he spoke as if to the devil himself. 'Are you playing tricks on me by putting savage Indians in my way? But hey, I did not survive the shipwreck to be frightened by a four-legged creature!'

Caliban's gabardine wasn't large enough to cover either him or Trinculo entirely, and both their legs remained visible, leading Stephano to believe that the creature in front of his eyes was an indigenous monster with four legs. So when he heard Caliban speak his language, he was terribly surprised. Enterprising as he was, the butler immediately realised what a fine present this intelligible monster would make for any emperor, and decided to provide him some relief from his fit. He needed the creature to be healthy enough for the journey back to Naples.

This four-legged monster was of course the product of Stephano's delusion, and the fit was actually the false impression the butler had got from Trinculo and Caliban's movements under the gabardine.

Again Caliban cried, 'Do not torment me, I pray you! I will bring your wood home faster.'

Stephano thought the monster was speaking gibberish in his delirium, and decided to give the creature some of his liquor. 'Come, open your mouth,' Stephano said, touching his bottle to Caliban's lips. 'This will put an end to your trembling.'

Trinculo recognised Stephano's voice. He exclaimed, 'But I am certain he is drowned. It must have been the devil who just spoke!'

'Four legs and two voices,' said the butler, hearing a

second voice come from under the gabardine, as the situation grew more and more farcical. 'A most delicate monster! I must cure him of his ague with the help of this bottle.' And he poured more wine in Caliban's mouth.

'Stephano!' Trinculo cried, and this time put all the confusion to rest. 'Speak to me if you be him, and don't be afraid, for I am Trinculo, your good friend.'

'Come forth, if you speak the truth,' Stephano said, and pulled the jester by his legs. 'You are Trinculo indeed! Have you been excreted by this creature of misshapen birth?'

'Oh no, I thought he had been killed by lightning,' Trinculo corrected his friend, 'so I took shelter from the storm under his gabardine. But you must tell me how you escaped the shipwreck. O Stephano, we are two Neapolitans alive!'

Caliban had taken well to the liquor. While the reunited friends marvelled at their survival, Caliban found himself filled with reverence for Stephano, who had provided him with what he thought was a celestial drink. 'I will swear upon that bottle to be your true subject,' he said to the butler. 'Have you come from heaven?'

'Out of the moon, I promise,' Stephano joked. 'I used to be the man in the moon in fact.'

Caliban had grown credulous under the influence of alcohol. 'Then I have seen you inside the moon,' he told Stephano, 'and adored you from the earth. I learnt about you from my mistress, who pointed my eyes in your direction. And there you were, with your dog by your side, and the thorn bush in your hands.'

Caliban's wine-induced deference provided Stephano with great enjoyment, but Trinculo wasn't amused. 'A most gullible monster he is for believing in these tall tales,' he remarked.

But Trinculo's words held no significance for Caliban, who was already making promises to show Stephano every fertile inch of the island and take him to the best springs that flowed on it. 'I will pluck you berries,' he said, 'catch fish for you and fetch you wood. A plague on the tyrant I serve! Never again shall I obey his orders, but follow you instead, O wondrous man.'

'A most ridiculous monster,' Trinculo thought, 'to take a drunkard for a wonder.'

But it wasn't a time to be reasonable when the smell of freedom was so near. 'No more fetching of firewood, no washing of dishes or catching fish for Prospero!' cried Caliban. Then he broke into a merry song, rejoicing at the thought of his imminent liberty.

> *Ban' ban' Ca-caliban,*
> *Has a new master, get a new man.*
> *Freedom, high-day; high-day freedom; freedom high-day, freedom.*

Drunk and misguided, Caliban looked forward to a fresh

lease of life, and led the way for Stephano and his friend, tottering towards the island's delights.

# 3

There are tasks that are wretched, but if performed with dignity, often such labours bring satisfaction and good fortune. So Ferdinand, under Prospero's orders, carried logs on his shoulders and thought of Miranda, a thought powerful enough to make his task seem pleasurable. 'She is ten times more gentle than her father,' he said to himself.

Prospero had asked Ferdinand to collect a large number of logs and pile them up for him. Watching him toil ceaselessly moved Miranda to tears. 'I beg you, don't work so hard,' she said. 'Set the logs down and rest for a while. My father is engrossed in his books; you needn't worry about him. Let me carry the wood for you.'

But how could Ferdinand let her do such dishonourable work? 'No, precious creature,' he said. 'I would rather that my muscles cracked and my back broke than you go through such trouble.'

'I could do the work as well as you,' Miranda asserted, 'even better in fact, because I am more willing to do it than you are.'

In this way they continued to argue, oblivious to Prospero's presence, who was standing at a distance and watching the scene with satisfaction.

'Let me finish what I started,' Ferdinand told Miranda. 'When you are near me, the night feels like a fresh morning, and my tasks seem less difficult. And yet I am not even aware of your name. Do tell me what it is, so I can include it in my prayers.'

Prospero had asked Miranda not to submit to Ferdinand's requests, but still she told him her name.

As their attraction grew stronger, Ferdinand recalled how he had regarded many women with affection before. But not one of them But not one of them could compare with Miranda, whose every feature was unrivalled.

'I cannot say what features women have beyond this island,' Miranda told him. 'The only woman I know is myself. Nor have I met any man other than you and my father. But I do know that it is only for you I want to preserve my virginity.' But then she remembered her father's instructions and stopped herself short; she had already said much more than Prospero would have liked.

Ferdinand began to speak in turn, and told Miranda that he was a prince, and would never suffer the hardships

Prospero had put him through. But his heart had been enslaved the moment he had set eyes on her, and it was for her sake that he had agreed to undergo those pains.

'Do you love me?' Miranda asked him.

'I do prize and honour you,' he said, 'and my love for you knows no bounds.'

These words touched Miranda so deeply that she began to think herself unworthy of the love Ferdinand had professed for her. 'I will be your wife if you marry me,' she said, 'but if you don't I will die your maid. You may refuse marriage with me, but I will stay by your side as a servant even if it is against your wish.'

'I want to marry you as desperately as bondage longs for freedom,' Ferdinand said, and gave Miranda his hand.

She had disobeyed her father's commands, but Prospero wasn't upset. He had heard the lovers express their sincere feelings for each other, and there was nothing that could make Prospero happier. Things were going according to plan, and his daughter was now engaged to the Prince of Naples. But there were other tasks to be performed, so Prospero returned to his books to make preparations for their union.

***

There was still liquor in the cask. So Stephano swore not to drink a drop of water till he ran out of wine. And he would not let his companions stay sober either. 'Servant-monster, drink up!' he said to Caliban, who still laboured under the impression that Stephano was a demi-god. 'Your eyes are almost set in your head,' the butler continued, noticing Caliban's inebriated state.

'Where else should his eyes be set?' remarked Trinculo, irritated by Stephano's foolish behaviour. 'He would be a valuable monster if he had eyes in his tail!'

But the drunken butler took no notice of Trinculo. 'My monster-friend has drowned himself in wine,' he said. 'But as for myself, not even the sea can drown me. Thirty-five leagues I swam till I finally made it to the shore. Having achieved this feat, I now declare this creature to be my trusted flag-bearer, my standard.'

But Caliban was in no position to stand, his stomach bursting with liquor. 'He could be your lieutenant maybe,' Trinculo pointed out, 'but by no means your standard.'

Trinculo's biting comments didn't please Caliban in the least. 'I shall not serve him,' he told Stephano. 'He's not valiant like you.'

'Ignorant monster!' Trinculo cried, also intoxicated by wine. 'I could jostle a constable if I tried. It is only because I am a valiant man that I could drink such a large quantity of wine today. But you are no man, merely half fish and half monster, and that is why you tell such monstrous lies about me!'

'Oh how he mocks me!' Caliban complained. 'Bite him to death, I pray you,' he said to Stephano.

Stephano told his cynical friend to choose his words carefully. 'If you rebel I will hang you like a mutineer from the next tree!' he threatened.

Now that Trinculo's unruly behaviour had been taken care of, Caliban asked the butler if he would listen to a request. He wanted to avenge Prospero for usurping the island from him and causing him torment ever since. And to this end, he wanted Stephano's help.

Once again Ariel was in the vicinity, and he overheard Caliban. Imitiating Trinculo's voice, he said, 'You lie!'

'You lie, you foolish monkey!' Caliban said to Trinculo, while Ariel remained invisible to everyone.

Stephano was enraged by what he thought was Trinculo's insolence. 'If you trouble him any more, I will remove some of your teeth!' he said.

'But I said nothing,' Trinculo promised sincerely.

'And say nothing more,' Stephano told him.

So Caliban continued with his suit. He told Stephano how Prospero had taken the island for himself by means of sorcery. 'Would your highness take revenge on him and get the island back?' he said. 'You will then be its master, and I your faithful servant.'

Having drunk to the bitter end, Stephano was out of ideas. 'And how exactly will we bring about this revenge?' he asked.

'I will lead you to his cell when he's asleep,' Caliban told the butler, 'and you may drive a nail into his head.'

Again Ariel faked the jester's voice and said, 'Another lie! You only make false claims.'

'Give him a few blows, master. Take the bottle from him,' Caliban said, pointing at Trinculo.

'But what have I done? The monster keeps accusing me for nothing,' Trinculo protested and went and stood sulkily at a distance.

With Trinculo standing away from the rest of his group, Ariel could no longer provoke the conspirators to argue amongst themselves. So with no further interruptions, Caliban told the butler that it was Prospero's habit to sleep in the afternoon. While he slept, they would take away his books, without which he was powerless. Stephano could then kill him any way he pleased—batter his skull with a log, stab him in the stomach, or even slit his throat with a knife. 'We must destroy his books,' Caliban repeated. 'By doing so we destroy the knowledge with which he uses his magical implements, of which he has many. And the best of them all is his beautiful daughter, who will become your wife when you are ruler of this island, and produce fine children for you.'

Stephano could not resist such temptations. 'I will certainly kill this man,' he said. 'His daughter and I shall be king and queen, and you and Trinculo my viceroys.'

Fully apprised of the plan against Prospero's life, Ariel made a mental note to report it to his master, as Caliban made merry. 'I am filled with pleasure,' he said, and asked Stephano to join him in singing the song he had sung when they had first met. But Stephano sang a different tune altogether.

*Flout 'em and scout 'em,*
*And scout 'em and flout 'em,*
*Thought is free.*

'That's not the tune you taught me,' said Caliban.

At that moment all three of them heard the tune as if being played on a tabor, but try as they might, they could not locate its source. This was of course Ariel's doing, who was using yet another means to distract the conspirators from their murderous plan.

'Who plays this music?' Stephano asked. 'Show yourself if you be a man. But if you are the devil, d … do what you will. Mercy upon us, for there is nothing we can do to stop you!'

Stephano was visibly afraid. So Caliban tried to console him. He told him how the island was full of unaccountable noises, sweet and delightful, but never bringing any harm. He recalled how various stringed instruments would sound sweetly in his ears, and melodious voices would bring sleep to his eyes. Often while he slept he would see the sky opening up to shower riches upon him. So fantastic were these visions that when he awoke he would long to sleep again.

'A fine kingdom this would prove to me,' Stephano said, moved by Caliban's account.

'Only when Prospero is destroyed,' Caliban reminded him. And before the island's rich offerings could distract Stephano again, Caliban led the way for him and Trinculo towards their enemy's cell.

***

The king's son was nowhere in sight. It had been hours since Alonso and his party had begun their search. Gonzalo's muscles were sore, and his bones ached from walking without pause. 'I can go no further,' he said. 'This island is nothing short of a maze.'

The king himself was seized by weariness. They had searched far and wide, and the little hope Gonzalo had revived in him was dying. So he resigned himself to fate and joined the councillor in resting.

Only Antonio saw an opportunity arising out of the king's exhaustion. He reminded Sebastian of their plan to murder him. 'Do not for one second forget our purpose,' he said to the king's brother. 'Let us execute our plan tonight itself, while they are still weakened by fatigue and thus incautious.' Sebastian nodded his agreement.

Suddenly strange music filled the air. Several mysterious creatures appeared, carrying a banquet. They set the table down daintily and danced a mystical dance around it, inviting the king and his troupe to eat. Then in the blink of an eye they were gone, leaving everyone astonished.

'My good friends, did you hear the enchanting sounds?' Alonso asked. 'Such marvellous music!' said Gonzalo.

Sebastian could not believe his eyes. 'This spectacle makes me think that unicorns do exist, that there are indeed phoenixes in Arabia!'

Antonio was of the same opinion. 'I will believe so too, and every other fantastic thing I've heard before. It seems travellers do not return to their homes to tell lies; it is the fools who stay inside who cannot see any truth in their stories.'

'But if I were to report this incident back in Naples, would the people there believe me?' Gonzalo wondered aloud. 'If I told them of the islanders I saw, mysteriously shaped, yet of manners more gentle than anyone from my nation …'

Prospero, who had conjured the banquet and instructed the spirits of the island to perform the spectacle, watched Alonso and the rest be overcome by amazement. Invisible to everyone, he listened to their remarks. What Gonzalo said reminded Prospero of the treachery he had undergone. 'My brave spirits are certainly made of gentle manners,' he thought, 'unlike some of you present here, who are worse than devils.'

The spirits had vanished, but the banquet remained, beckoning the hungry castaways. Sebastian suggested they taste the numerous dishes that lay on the table.

'Have faith, sir,' Gonzalo said to Alonso when he refused to eat the food. 'In our younger days, we would believe that there were strange people who lived in the mountains with folds of skin hanging from their necks. Or that there were such men whose heads were in their chests. Will you then not eat this food, which lies in front of your very eyes?'

Convinced, Alonso proceeded towards the table, and asked everyone else to follow. But before they could even touch the dishes, lightning bolted from the sky, and out of nowhere a harpy came flying towards them. It hovered right above the banquet and flapped its wings viciously, as the food disappeared just as magically as Prospero's spirits had done.

It was really Ariel who had come in a harpy's disguise, to remind Prospero's detractors of their misdeeds, to make them repent for their treachery. 'You are three men of sin,' he screamed, pointing with his wings at the king, his brother, and the usurping duke, 'whom destiny has caused the sea to belch up on an island which men do not inhabit. And on this island I have driven you insane.'

'You are fools,' Ariel continued, seeing the men draw their swords. 'The excessive courage you display will lead to your own destruction. I and my fellow creatures are ministers of fate; do you think you can stab us with your swords of steel? Put those useless things away and listen carefully to my words. From Milan you did supplant Duke Prospero, and exposed him and his innocent child to the sea. It is this grave offence that has vexed the sea and all its shores and every creature that lives there. For this reason you, Alonso, have lost your son. It is only a matter of time till damnation comes to each of you, stranded here on this desolate island, where life can only be full of penitence and sorrow.'

More thunder sounded, as Ariel in the harpy's guise, vanished in a flash. The spirits who had brought the banquet returned, and taking the empty table with them, they disappeared into the forest.

Prospero congratulated Ariel on his performance. 'Brave spirit, you have followed my instructions to the last detail. And so have the spirits who assisted you. My superior magic has worked its charms, and my enemies are now confused in their fit of temporary madness.' And leaving them in that state, Prospero went to visit Ferdinand and Miranda.

'Oh the monstrosity!' Alonso cried in utter bewilderment. 'The waves themselves spoke to me of my misdeed,' he said, filled with repentance. 'I heard the winds sing it to me, and it was as if the thunder itself pronounced Prospero's name.' Alonso blamed himself for Ferdinand's death in the tempest, and wished his own life would end so he could lie beneath the seabed next to his beloved son.

Seeing the three men in their mad, guilt-ridden state, Gonzalo asked those who were less affected by the recent happenings to stay close to their masters. They seemed to be on the verge of inflicting upon themselves horrendous acts of madness, and after all the terrible things that had come to pass, those at any cost had to be prevented.

# 4

Finally Ferdinand learnt the reason for the punishments he had had to suffer. His travails were only a test of his love—Prospero explained to him—and he had passed it well. He could now receive Miranda's hand in marriage, and with her father's blessing.

Happy that his hardships were over, Ferdinand smiled at his would be father-in-law. But he had smiled too soon. 'You have received as a gift from me a woman of superior value,' Prospero told him. 'But over time she will outdo even these high praises I sing of her, and then will it be a more appropriate time for you to smile.'

'I have no doubt that she will,' said Ferdinand.

A wedding ceremony was in order, but once again Prospero set him a condition. 'However, you may consummate the relationship only after your marriage is solemnised,' he said. 'If you fail to wait till the rites have been performed, there will be no peace in your lives, only bitterness and hatred, and no children to keep alive your name.'

But Ferdinand was steadfast in his honour. He promised that he would not let anything turn it into lust—no secret cave of the island, nor any suggestion of his imagination. So Prospero left the lovers to each other's company, and summoned his diligent servant.

'What is my next task, master?' said Ariel.

'There is another trick you must perform,' Prospero told him, 'with help from your subordinate spirits. Go bring them to this place, and tell them what their duties are. The betrothed couple expects to see a display of my magical skills.'

A pageant was to be performed, and Prospero explained to Ariel how he had imagined it. Ariel left to gather the spirits of the island and prepare them for the festivities.

Prospero was still afraid that Ferdinand might fail to keep his word and let his passion guide his actions. 'I warn you once more—abstain from taking my daughter's virginity,' he said, 'or you will not be allowed to take your marriage vows.'

'Sir, the chastity of my heart is so strong that it keeps my passions repressed,' assured Ferdinand.

This time Prospero did not doubt the honesty in his words, and called for the pageant to begin.

Soft music played around them as a spirit arrived gracefully, dressed as Iris, messenger of the gods. With great lyrical skill, she welcomed Ceres and Juno to be a part of the celebrations.

*Ceres, most bountiful lady, your rich leas,*

*Of wheat, rye, barley, vetches, oats and peas;*
*Your grassy mountains where live nibbling sheep,*
*And flat meads thatched with fodder them to keep;*
*Your pole-clipped vineyard,*
*Your seacoast, sterile and rocky-hard,*
*Where you air Juno, the queen of all the sky,*
*Whose rainbow-like messenger am I,*
*Approach as Juno's peacocks fly amain,*
*Approach rich Ceres, her to entertain.*

As a spirit in Juno's guise descended from the sky, another one dressed as Ceres approached, and asked Iris the reason for the festivities.

Iris continued:

*A contract of true love to celebrate,*
*A present generously to estate*
*On the blessed lovers.*

Juno suggested she and Ceres waste no time in blessing the couple. She began to sing a joyful song:

*Honour, riches, marriage-blessing,*
*Long continuance and increasing,*
*Hourly joys be still upon you;*
*Juno sings her blessings on you.*

It was Ceres' turn next. She sang:

*Earth's increase, abundance plenty,*
*Barns and garners never empty.*
*Vines with clustering bunches growing,*

*Plants with goodly burden bowing;*
*Spring come to you at the farthest,*
*At the end of autumn's harvest.*
*Scarcity and want shall shun you,*
*Ceres' blessing so is on you.*

'This is a most majestic vision!' Ferdinand exclaimed, wishing he could live on the island forever.

Happy to see Ferdinand so captivated by the performance, Prospero explained to him how by means of his magical powers he had called on the island's spirits to enact the pageant. And the celebrations had only just begun.

Taking charge again, Iris now called to the nymphs that lived in the brooks and invited them to join in the merriment. Next she invited farmers to dance in pairs with these graceful naiads. In an instant arrived spirits dressed like reapers and harvesters, and each farmer took a nymph for a partner and joined with her in a rustic dance.

Miranda and Ferdinand were enjoying themselves thoroughly. But Prospero had been so engrossed in the celebrations that something important had slipped his mind. Suddenly he remembered that a conspiracy against his life was under way. He exclaimed aloud, breaking the spell, as confusion ensued among the spirits. The festivities came to an abrupt end, and the spirits sadly took their leave and vanished into thin air.

Ferdinand noticed the concern on Prospero's face and

said to Miranda, 'Your father is greatly affected by something.'

'I have never seen him so troubled,' she said in agreement.

Prospero felt that he had upset the couple by ending the pageant so suddenly. He thought Ferdinand looked disheartened, so he tried to console him. 'Be cheerful, sir. The revels had to end sometime. The actors you saw were all spirits, and they have now melted into thin air, just like the fleeting illusions they conjured—the cloud-capped towers, the gorgeous palaces, the solemn temples. The great globe itself will one day dissolve with everyone on it, and like the pageant, leave not a trace behind. We are not any different from our dreams either—forgotten when our time is up, our little lives coming to a close as we fall into the endless sleep of death.'

The pageant couldn't have been merrier, Miranda would soon be Naples' heiress, and reconciliation was waiting round the corner. Yet something troubled Prospero, something inexplicable even to himself. 'Do bear with my mind's weaknesses,' he said to Ferdinand, realising his thoughts had gone astray. 'My old brain is troubled, and I prattle things of no concern to you. If you so wish, retire to my cell and rest awhile. I will take a short walk and calm my troubled mind.'

When Ferdinand and Miranda had left him by himself, Prospero called to Ariel and told him that they must foil Caliban's plan for murder. 'Where did you last see those scoundrels?' he asked.

Ariel had found the conspirators in a state of inebriation.

They were so inflamed by alcohol that they struck at the air for surrounding them and beat the ground for touching their feet from below. Then Ariel had played on his tabor, and charming their ears, led them through trails covered with prickly shrubs, and brought them to a filthy pond near Prospero's cell. Into this pond they had jumped and danced unmindfully, only the putrid water smelling worse than their unclean feet.

Prospero was pleased to hear of their misfortunes. But the drunks were yet to be caught. So he asked Ariel to fetch some gaudy garments from his cell, with which they would decoy the threesome.

'A devil, a born devil,' Prospero said, thinking of Caliban, 'whose nature no amount of nurture can change. The pains I took to teach him to be human have all come to nothing. And as his body grows uglier with age, so does his mind. Now the only thing left to do is plague him and his pesky friends.'

Even while he spoke, Caliban came with Stephano and Trinculo in tow, all three of them dripping wet. Stephano was growing impatient. 'Only a short while now, my lord,' Caliban placated him. 'The prize I will lead you to will compensate for our adversities.'

But losing their liquor bottles in the pond had made the men indignant. 'I will fetch my bottle,' Stephano declared, 'even though I may have to be over my ears in water for it.'

As Caliban pleaded with him to be quiet, Trinculo

noticed the clothes that Ariel had left on the ground. 'O King Stephano!' he shouted. 'Look, a wardrobe fit for you!'

'Leave it be, you fool,' Caliban told him, irritated. 'It's nothing but trash.'

But Trinculo was already trying on one of the gowns. Caliban was afraid the noise would wake Prospero from his afternoon sleep. 'If we run out of time, that cruel sorcerer will turn us into barnacles and apes!'

Stephano and the jester paid him no heed. They heaped the garments on Caliban's arms and ordered him to carry them to the place where they had stored their wine. 'Or I'll turn you out of my kingdom!' Stephano yelled drunkenly.

He only stopped to listen when the shouts of hunters came to their ears. The spirits had taken the shape of hounds, as Prospero and Ariel set them on the threesome. Seeing the dogs come after them, they ran helter-skelter.

'Fury! Tyrant!' yelled Prospero to the dogs. 'Grind their joints and cramp their muscles. Make them more spotted than mountain cats!'

As the chasers and the chased disappeared into the distance, Prospero sighed. His enemies were at his mercy. Soon Ariel's labours would come to an end and he would have his freedom. There was only one thing left to do.

The time had come for the revelations.

# 5

In the linden grove near Prospero's cell, the King of Naples sat dismayed. His brother Sebastian stood with Antonio, still dazed from their encounter with the harpy. The rest of the entourage despaired of their situation, and tears ran down Gonzalo's cheeks as he watched the king in his maddened state.

'They're prisoners of your spell, master,' Ariel reported to Prospero. 'If you saw them now, your heart would surely soften.'

Though their crimes and treachery had filled Prospero with vengeance, he believed it was nobler to forgive. 'With the wrongdoers repenting for their misdeeds, my cause for revenge has ceased to exist,' he said. 'Release them, Ariel. It is time I lifted my charms and restored their senses.'

Prospero prepared to reveal himself to his friends and foes of twelve years past. With his staff he traced a circle on the ground. He called out to the elves that lived on hills and in the brooks, the fairies that made ringlets in the grass under night's cover, and the spirits that rejoiced at the curfew hour whose bell declared them free to roam the earth till the sun rose again. To these helpers Prospero said, 'With your aid I have caused the sun to eclipse, made tempests roar, rifted trees with thunderbolts. Sleepers from their graves have risen in answer to my magical spells, hills have quaked in response. But today I vow to relinquish my power, to break my staff and bury it deep in the earth, and drown my books in the sea.'

Music played as Ariel came, drawing the king and his men into the circle. Prospero observed them after all those years, as they stood charmed, unable to see or hear him. 'Bring my hat and rapier from my cell,' he said to Ariel, and the airy spirit returned with the items in a trice. Prospero disrobed, and for the first time in twelve years he appeared in his ducal attire. He then sent Ariel to the ship to wake the master and the boatswain and bring them to him.

By this time the spell had broken, and Gonzalo, finding himself able to speak again, wished some heavenly power would guide them out of the frightening island.

But they found to their horror that they had unknowingly entered a magical circle which held them captive. Prospero came before them and said, 'Behold the wronged Duke of Milan!'

The king's party stared at him in disbelief. For assurance's sake, Prospero embraced the king and welcomed him with cheer.

'I cannot tell if you are Prospero or an apparition that has come to haunt me,' said Alonso, mustering all the courage he had. 'But you seem to be made of flesh and blood. And since I saw you, my afflicted mind has healed.' Alonso asked to hear the explanations behind all the strange occurrences they had recently witnessed. But before anything else, he would have Prospero tell him how he had survived all these years and on that island.

But the story could wait; first Prospero owed the kind councillor a debt of gratitude. He held Gonzalo in his arms and said, 'So great is your heart that its honour can be neither measured nor confined.'

Next he addressed Sebastian and Antonio and told them he had received knowledge of their plot to assassinate the king, and he could bring down the king's anger on them if he so wished. But luckily for them, his intention was not to punish.

With Antonio's treachery still fresh in his memory, it was difficult for Prospero to call him brother. Yet he forgave him, and told Antonio that he had no choice but to return the dukedom as its rightful duke was still living—even the king had so decreed.

Alonso could still not bring himself to believe that the Prospero before him was real. 'Share with us the details of your survival,' he demanded. 'Tell us by what coincidence we have met, as it has been only three hours since we were shipwrecked upon this shore and the cruel waters claimed my son.'

Prospero said he had lost his daughter too, but unlike the king, he had patiently accepted his fate.

'A daughter?' It had been so long that Alonso had forgotten Prospero had a child. 'How did you lose her?'

'I lost her to the same tempest that you were in,' said Prospero, as it was the storm that had brought Ferdinand to the island, where he met and got engaged to Miranda.

Prospero noticed that the other men were still staring at him in amazement, thinking their eyes were deceiving them. So he told them yet again that he was indeed the duke who was deported from Milan, who landed on the shore of this island to be its ruler instead.

But he would share no more, as his story was not one meant to be told over a meal, but a chronicle to be narrated over days. So he welcomed the king into his cell and promised to delight him as much as he had delighted Prospero by returning him his dukedom.

Alonso's delight knew no bounds when he saw Ferdinand, alive and well, sitting inside Prospero's cell and playing chess with his betrothed.

Once again Alonso could hardly believe his eyes. 'If this is only an illusion, my one son I will lose twice.'

But Ferdinand had already seen his father at the mouth of the cell. Overcome with happiness, he came towards Alonso and knelt.

'You have all the blessings of an overjoyed father,' said Alonso, helping him up. 'Now tell me how you came to this island and made the acquaintance of this maiden.' Like his son, even Alonso mistook Miranda to be the island's goddess.

Ferdinand corrected him. 'She is mortal, sir, but by immortal providence she is mine.' He told Alonso that he had chosen her for his wife without his father's permission, thinking him to be dead. 'She is daughter to the famous Duke of Milan,' he continued, 'of whom I have often heard but never saw before.'

Guilt-ridden for having unknowingly made his future daughter-in-law suffer, Alonso asked Miranda for forgiveness. 'Give me your hands,' he said to the couple, 'and let those who do not wish you joy suffer grief and sorrow.'

Joy was in the air indeed. 'Such wonderful creatures there are in this world,' Miranda exclaimed on meeting for the first time in years so many of her kind.

At this point, the master and the boatswain arrived, eyes wide with wonder. 'Look!' cried Gonzalo. 'There's more of our party! Hadn't I prophesied that this boatswain could never drown?'

The boatswain was glad to be reunited with the king and his men. He informed them that the ship was safe in harbour, as splendid and seaworthy as when it had first set sail. He told them how every member of the crew had found himself asleep under the deck, and was wakened by shrieks and howls and the sounds of jangling chains. And then in an instant he and the master had been separated from the rest of the crew and brought magically to this place.

'Well done, my diligent spirit,' Prospero said to Airel. 'You shall have your freedom soon.' Pleased to hear this, Ariel left to find Caliban and his companions and bring them before his master.

There were still two men missing from the king's company. Prospero pointed to Stephano and Trinculo, as Ariel returned, driving them and their new friend on.

The alcohol's effect was wearing off. Caliban took in the sight in front of him, and thinking the men to be wonderful spirit-friends of his master, realised Prospero was indeed powerful. He feared he would be severely punished, pinched to death even, so he vowed to be obedient and asked Prospero to have mercy on him. 'What a fool I was to take a dull drunkard for a god,' he admitted.

Prospero introduced Caliban to the king as the deformed son of a witch who could control even the moon and the tides. He told Alonso of this creature's plot to take Prospero's life, a plot in which the king's servants were his willing accomplices. 'And since you would like me to take pity on you,' Prospero said, turning to Caliban, 'go to my cell with your companions and decorate it nicely.'

In this cell Prospero requested the king and his party to rest their weary minds and muscles, and promised to relate to them the story of his life since he came to live on the island. The next morning he would take them to their ship, and everyone would return to Naples, where Prospero hoped to see his daughter and Alonso's son wedded.

To this end he made a sincere promise. 'You may now look forward to calm waters, favourable winds and a journey so smooth that soon we will be sailing next to the royal fleet from which you became separated.'

And after this final task did Ariel get his liberty, Caliban his island, Ferdinand and Miranda each other, Prospero his dukedom—and if this formidable duke were to be believed—everyone else their just deserts.

# Supplementary Reading

# Character Sketches

## PROSPERO

With his awe-inspiring stature, his expertise in the magical arts, and the power he wields over almost everyone in *The Tempest*, Prospero is undoubtedly the play's central character.

Early in the play we learn that Prospero's dukedom has been usurped by his treacherous brother Antonio. At this point Prospero certainly earns our sympathy, banished from his own state to live on an unknown island with his three-year-old daughter. While Antonio turns Prospero's followers against him, we come to know that he isn't entirely successful, that Prospero did have at least one loyal supporter. On the night of Prospero's banishment, the old councillor Gonzalo secretly furnishes him with food, clothes and the books he valued above everything else.

When Prospero reaches the island, the only thing at his disposal is his knowledge of sorcery, an art he had dedicated all his time to, naively trusting his brother with the governance of the duchy. But Prospero learns from his mistake, and on the island where he comes to live, he is relentless. According to Caliban's account, in his early days on the island Prospero used him to his advantage, and later enslaved him by means of his magic and proclaimed himself ruler of the territory.

Although Prospero denies most of Caliban's accusations, we are never sure whom to believe. In fact, Prospero's plan of revenge, the sufferings he makes King Alonso and his men undergo, and the painful punishments he metes out to Caliban, do not paint a favourable picture of the wronged duke. While he takes pride in his own magical skills and considers them harmless, he can only cast aspersions on Caliban's witch-mother Sycorax, and decries her for being able to control the moon and the tides. Prospero wants to avenge his brother and the king for taking his dukedom through unlawful means, but never feels guilty for having usurped from Caliban the island that rightfully belonged to him.

By the end of the play however, all issues are resolved. Antonio is compelled to return to Prospero his dukedom, Ariel is freed from his service, and Caliban is master of his island once again. Prospero has a change of heart—instead of seeking the revenge he had initially planned, he forgives everyone and looks forward to Miranda and Ferdinand's wedding, which suggests his desire for a harmonious relationship with the King of Naples who was once his enemy.

Throughout the play, Prospero betrays qualities both agreeable and otherwise, and it is this indeterminacy of his character that makes him one of Shakespeare's most significant creations.

## CALIBAN

On multiple occasions in the play and from multiple characters we hear that Caliban is a deformed savage, a creature only half human, whom it is easy to abhor. It is established time and again that his appearance is ugly, and his mind equally detestable. Miranda tells Ferdinand that he and Prospero are the only two men she has ever seen, thus refusing to acknowledge that Caliban is human. To Trinculo and Stephano he is nothing more than a useful monster, a strange islander who will make for an exotic gift to any emperor in Europe.

But Caliban corroborates these claims only partially. He does not deny that he had attempted to rape Miranda, but he never makes a clear admission either. He does wish to murder Prospero, and with Stephano and Trinculo hatches a plan against his life. But it is clear that this is his reaction to the years of punishment Prospero has made him suffer and the hateful tasks he constantly performs under his master's orders. Caliban's murderous plan and his constant curses do not logically indicate an innate vileness, even though that is what Miranda would like to believe.

Caliban also mentions the various ways in which he came to Prospero's aid when the latter first set foot on the island. And although he is not repaid in a gracious way, Caliban is incredulous enough to repeat his acts of kindness when Stephano pours wine in his mouth, which intoxicates him into believing that the drunken butler is a 'wondrous man', a demi-god. Once again we are led to believe that it is his inclination to trust strangers too quickly and not a race-induced evilness that causes Caliban to suffer punishment, slavery and exploitation.

## MIRANDA

For the better part of the play, Miranda is depicted as an innocent, wide-eyed girl, guided completely by her father, who engineers her first meeting with Ferdinand and ensures that she falls in love with him. In relation to Miranda, Prospero is very much a conservative patriarch; twice he warns Ferdinand against taking her virginity before their marriage is solemnised. In turn, Miranda, by being engaged to Ferdinand, unknowingly ensures that Prospero's enmity with Ferdinand's father, the King of Naples, will end. In this way she becomes Prospero's vehicle for achieving one of his chief objectives. Miranda thus serves two main purposes—of a useful daughter, and a beautiful future wife who will guarantee the continuance of her husband's and her father's lineage.

But there are instances in the play in which Miranda comes across as forthright instead of submissive and docile. She goes against her father's commands and meets Ferdinand secretly. She even reveals her name in spite of

Prospero's warnings. Assuming her father to be asleep, Miranda asks Ferdinand to let her do the task Prospero had ordered him to perform. And when Caliban jeers at them, Miranda harangues him for being ungrateful, paying no heed to the codes of decorum women of her time were expected to follow.

Even though her acts of assertion are far outnumbered by the instances that show her to be the epitome of chastity and womanly goodness, Miranda, like her father, remains an ambivalent character.

# Questions

## 1

a. Who is Gonzalo? Why does he think the ship he is on will not sink in the tempest?

b. Who has brought about this tempest? What does he say about his past to his daughter?

c. Why does Ariel think he should be freed from his master's service? From what torments had his master freed him twelve years ago?

d. Who is Caliban? What reasons does he give for the displeasure he feels towards Prospero?

e. Why does Ferdinand agree to follow Prospero's orders? Why does Prospero want to punish him?

## 2

a. Whose loss is Alonso mourning? What does Francisco say to comfort him?

b. What do Antonio and Sebastian plan to do while the rest of their group is asleep?

c. If Gonzalo were king of the island he is stranded on, how would he govern it?

d. Why does Sebastian blame Alonso for their current situation?
e. What does Caliban promise to do for Stephano? Why does he think Stephano is a 'wondrous man'?

**3**

a. What has Prospero ordered Ferdinand to do? How does Miranda plan to relieve him?
b. How does Miranda go against her father's wishes?
c. What does Caliban promise Stephano if he killed Prospero and became the master of the island?
d. When Stephano feels afraid on hearing Ariel play on his tabor, how does Caliban comfort him? What does he say about the island?
e. What does Ariel, in a harpy's disguise, say to the king, his brother and Antonio? What is Alonso's reaction?

**4**

a. Why had Prospero been punishing Ferdinand? What does he offer him as a reward?
b. What warning does Prospero give Ferdinand? What is Ferdinand's reply?
c. Which are the three goddesses that play a part in the pageant? What does Prospero suddenly remember while the pageant is still in progress?

d. What does Prospero tell Ferdinand after the pageant has ended?
e. Where and in what condition had Ariel last seen Caliban and his companions? How do Ariel and Prospero chase them away?

**5**

a. After calling out to the spirits of the island, what does Prospero vow to do?
b. How does Prospero appear in front of Alonso and his men? What does he do to assure Alonso that he is indeed the wronged Duke of Milan? What is Alonso's reaction?
c. Why does Prospero praise Gonzalo? What does he say next to Antonio and Sebastian? Does he forgive them?
d. What does Alonso do when he finds out that his son is engaged to Prospero's daughter?
e. How does Prospero introduce Caliban? What does he ask Caliban and his companions to do for him?
f. What promise does Prospero finally make to Alonso? What do you think Prospero will do once he returns to Italy?

# *Much Ado About Nothing*

William Shakespeare

**Retold by**
**Lasantha Rodrigo**

# *Characters*

Don Pedro, *prince of Aragon*

Benedick, *a young lord of Padua*

Leonato, *governor of Messina*

Hero, *daughter to Leonato*

Beatrice, *niece to Leonato, and cousin to Hero*

Antonio, *father to Beatrice*

Claudio, *a young lord of Florence*

Don John, *illegitimate brother to Don Pedro*

Conrad, *a follower to Don John*

Borachio, *another follower to Don John*

Margaret, *one of the gentlewomen (maidservants) to Hero*

Ursula, *another maidservant*

Dogberry, *chief policeman*

Verges, *his deputy*

Balthasar, *a musician*

Friar Francis

Other messengers, watch, attendants

# 1

In the Italian town of Messina, the wealthy and kindly Leonato, the governor of Messina, received a letter from a messenger, stating that Don Pedro, the prince of Aragon, an old friend of his, was on his way to Messina after winning a battle. Count Claudio, Benedick, and Don John, the illegitimate brother of Don Pedro, were also with him, the letter said. According to the messenger, they had not lost any men in battle. Leonato was very glad to hear this news. He exclaimed in great jubilation, 'A victory is twice itself when the achiever brings home full numbers.'

Leonato also expressed his wonderment at the young Florentine, Claudio, who had fought in the battle. The messenger informed Leonato that the Florentine was held in high respect by both Don Peter and Don Pedro. He added, 'He has borne himself beyond the promise of his age, performing, in the figure of a lamb, the feats of a lion.' When Leonato said that Claudio had an uncle in Messina, the messenger told him that he had already delivered him letters and that the uncle had shed tears of happiness at the news.

At this point, Beatrice, Leonato's niece, inquired if Signor Mountanto had returned from battle, too. The messenger, however, did not know anyone by that name, so Leonato's daughter, Hero, explained that Beatrice was referring to Signor Benedick of Padua.

When the messenger informed Beatrice that Benedick had indeed returned, she asked in jest, 'Please tell me, how many has he killed and eaten in these wars? Or just how many has he killed? I promised him I would eat anyone he killed.'

Beatrice's further comments on Benedick revealed a vitriolic spirit, and Leonato told the messenger, 'Please don't take my niece the wrong way, sir. Benedick and Beatrice have been waging a war of wits between themselves. Whenever they meet, they battle it out.' When the messenger observed aloud that Benedick was not in Beatrice's good books, she replied, 'No; and if he were, I would burn my study.' She asked the messenger who Benedick's newest companion was, and minced no words in describing the former. 'He wears his faith like his hats,' she said. 'It changes at every block.' The messenger responded, saying that it was the noble Claudio that Benedick was spending his time with.

At this juncture, Don Pedro approached with his illegitimate brother, Don John, Benedick and Claudio. Don Pedro's servant Balthasar followed them. Banter ensued upon their welcome. When Beatrice entered the conversation with a sarcastic remark at Benedick, he replied, 'What, my dear Lady Disdain! Are you still alive?' This brought on several exchanges between them, both launching fiery witticisms at each other. Beatrice continued to be sarcastic: 'Courtesy itself must turn into disdain, if you come in her presence.'

From their exchange it soon became clear that Benedick was forsworn to love. He told Beatrice, 'I wish I did not have such a hard heart; for, truly, I love none.' Beatrice's answer revealed that she was equally forsworn to love: 'I thank God and my cold blood that I am as opposed to love as you are.' Benedick and Beatrice kept hurling insults at each other, continuing to display their rivalry. Then Don Pedro announced to Claudio and Benedick that Leonato had invited them all to stay with him for a month, hoping some event would detain them even longer. Leonato extended a warm welcome to Don John, saying that he owed him all his duty as he and his brother, Don Pedro, had reconciled with each other.

When Benedick and Claudio were alone, the latter asked Benedick if he had taken note of Leonato's daughter. 'Is she not a modest young lady?' he asked. Benedick replied, 'She's too short to be praised highly, too dark to be praised fairly, and too small to be praised greatly.' Benedick further said that if she looked any different from what she did, she would be ugly, and since she couldn't be anything other than what she was, he didn't like her.'

Claudio entreated Benedick to be earnest in his reply, and Benedick realised that Claudio was indeed mesmerised by Hero. After expressing his own cynical thoughts on love and women, Benedick told Claudio, 'I'm still young enough to see without glasses, and I don't see what you're talking about. If her cousin Beatrice didn't have such a nasty temper, she'd be so much more beautiful than Hero that it would be fair enough to say that she is May while Hero is December.' He then asked Claudio, 'I hope you have no intent to turn husband, have you?' To this, Claudio replied, 'I would hardly trust myself, even if I had sworn the contrary, if Hero would be my wife.' Benedick responded with recrimination against love and marriage: 'Shall I never see a bachelor of sixty again?'

When Don Pedro entered and asked why Claudio and Benedick didn't follow him to Leonato's, Benedick at once replied that Claudio was in love with Leonato's daughter. Don Pedro responded, 'Amen, if you love her; for the lady is very well worthy.' Benedick couldn't restrain his words: 'I neither feel how she should be loved nor know how she should be worthy, and this is an opinion that fire cannot melt out of me.'

'You have always been an obstinate heretic about beauty,' remarked Don Pedro. Ultimately, Benedick revealed that he was determined to die a bachelor, but Don Pedro said that he would see, before he died, that Benedick would, indeed, fall in love.

Benedick, however, was adamant about his resolution: 'With anger, with sickness, or with hunger, my lord,' he said, 'not with love.' He claimed he could never be so much in love that a round of drinks would not be able to revive him.

Don Pedro said, 'In time the savage bull does bear the yoke.' And Benedick's quick reply was, 'The savage bull may; but if ever the sensible Benedick bear it, pluck off the bull's horns and set them in my forehead; and let me be vilely painted, and in such great letters as they write "Here is a good horse to hire," let them signify under my sign "Here you may see Benedick, the married man." '

Once these fiery exchanges ended, Don Pedro asked Benedick to tell Leonato that they would not fail him at supper, which Leonato had thoroughly prepared. When Benedick left to convey this message, Claudio entreated Don Pedro saying, 'My Lord, please help me now.' Don Pedro confirmed his allegiance to Claudio, saying, 'I am at your service. Just tell me what you want me to do, and however hard it is, you'll see that I'm eager to do it.' Claudio asked if Leonato had a son, to which Don Pedro replied in the negative, telling him that Hero was Leonato's only heir. Claudio then confided in Don Pedro his feelings for Hero. He mentioned that even though he had noticed her before the war, he had a rougher task in hand than to indulge in love at the time. But, now that he had returned, war-related thoughts had left their place vacant, and soft and delicate desires had come to take their place, all prompting him to think of how fair young Hero was and making him believe that he had liked her even before he had gone to war.

To Claudio's great relief, Don Pedro replied, 'If you do love fair Hero, cherish your love, and I will break the news to her and her father, and you shall then have her.' Don Pedro told Claudio of his plan: he would disguise himself as Claudio, since Claudio would be inhibited by his shyness, and woo Hero, and after winning her heart, he would tell Leonato of their love, and thus Hero would be Claudio's.

***

It was quite a turn of events when old Antonio, Leonato's brother, told Leonato that a man of his had overheard the prince talking to Claudio, confiding in the latter his intention of expressing his love for Leonato's daughter. Leonato wasn't sure how reliable the messenger's tale was, but Antonio assured him that the boy who reported the conversation was a good, sharp fellow. Leonato, however, using his good sense and judgement, told Antonio that he would simply hold the information as a dream until it manifested itself in reality. He added that he would give his daughter the news so that she could be better prepared when the prince proposed to her.

Leonato's house, in the meantime, was becoming a busy place, in preparation for the night's revelries.

It was customary in these times to entertain guests by hosting lavish masquerade balls. The young and beautiful men and women were thus about to embark on a month of festivities, and little did they know that very soon, their sense of love and duty, and their convictions, were about to face a series of challenges.

***

Don John, conversed with his companion, Conrade who asked Don John why he looked sad. Don John's response was, of course, in keeping with his villainous disposition. He told Conrade that he could not hide what he truly was and that he would look sad when he felt sad and laugh at no man's jokes, eat when he was hungry without waiting for any man, sleep when he'd be so inclined without worrying about anyone, and laugh when he felt merry and not to please someone.

Don John's hatred for his brother, became evident when he told Conrade that he would rather be a wild rose in a hedge than a rose in Don Pedro's grace. He advised Conrade to let him be what he was, rather than seeking to change his mood. At this, his equally villainous friend asked Don John whether his unhappiness was of any use—in other words, whether his mood could stir further villainous behaviour. It was at this moment that Borachio, a follower of Don John, entered the conversation, bringing news of a great opportunity for villainous schemes.

Borachio informed them that he had just returned from a great supper that Leonato had hosted. He also broke the news of an intended marriage. When Borachio revealed that the marriage was between Claudio and Hero, Don John, the conniving listener, immediately recognised a great opportunity for his villainy. Borachio informed them that he had been perfuming a musty room when Don Pedro and Claudio had come to his notice. He had hidden himself behind a tapestry, and listened to their confidential exchange. The prince, said Borachio, was going to woo Hero, pretending to be Claudio, and upon winning her, would give her over to Claudio.

This was enough for Don John to summon his two villainous counterparts to join him in making use of this opportunity to plan dark deeds. His intention was to harm Claudio, who, according to Don John, had enjoyed 'all the glory' at his overthrow.

Thus, the joviality of our formerly introduced charming characters, it seemed, was going to be tarnished by the schemes of some wily men.

# 2

The guests had had supper at Leonato's house, and they came out, wearing masks. It was customary in this era to wear masks at festivities for anonymity and therefore, freer conversation. Leonato, Antonio, Beatrice, and Hero noticed that John Pedro was not at supper. Also, Beatrice and Hero noticed that Don John had a morose look about him. In the conversation that followed, Beatrice said that she would live in heaven and have fun with the bachelors there forever.

When the revellers entered in pairs, Don Pedro asked Hero if she would dance with him, possibly to woo her on Claudio's behalf. Meanwhile, Margaret and Balthasar entered together, but Margaret rejected Balthasar's advances of love. Ursula reproached Antonio for being a dirty old man when he claimed to be someone else under the mask, but Ursula knew for sure that it was Antonio.

When Benedick, claiming to be someone else, asked Beatrice who Benedick was, Beatrice hurled insults at Benedick and informed him that Benedick was nothing but the prince's jester, 'a dull fool'. Don John and Borachio, with evil intent, told Benedick that Don Pedro was in love with Hero and that he was going to marry her the same night. Claudio was shattered by the news and tried to avoid Benedick, who spoke about the prince, Don Pedro, winning Hero for himself. Claudio eventually left and Benedick pondered over the reason for his friend's melancholy spirit, when Don Pedro joined him and asked where Claudio was. Benedick, in a somewhat playful manner, accused Don Pedro of 'stealing' Claudio's love interest, but Don Pedro was able to set things straight at once by informing Claudio that he had wooed and won Hero for Claudio and that he had also informed Leonato about the same. As Leonato himself was present among them and could confirm the news, the marriage could take place between Claudio and Hero any time. Claudio was at once cheerful again.

Meanwhile, Beatrice, in jest, lamented that she did not want to remain a maiden as Hero was also engaged now. She asked Don Pedro if he had any brother who might be interested in marrying her. When Don Pedro asked Beatrice if she would accept him, she refused and left the crowd to attend to matters Leonato had told her to look into. In her absence, Don Pedro appreciated her humour and joviality and asked everyone's assistance in bringing Beatrice and Benedick together. He said that he would give directions to everyone as to how his plan was to be executed. Everyone agreed to support the prince in his mission. Leonato and Don Pedro also persuaded Claudio to wait for a week before marrying Hero, so that Leonato could make all the arrangements the way he would like to.

Beatrice and Benedick were both intelligent and young. Don Pedro told the others the qualities that Benedick had, and if they succeeded in bringing the two together, they could then consider themselves as love gods. Their conviction to be forsworn to love, however, brought out a more mature and perhaps bitter perception of the world. Don Pedro, Leonato, Claudio, and Hero, their good-natured friends, would try their best to bring Benedick and Beatrice together.

***

The evil Don John was not at peace with the happenings taking place around him. When he told Borachio that Count Claudio's marriage to Hero was already fixed, Borachio at once presented a villainous plan to thwart the marriage. He told Don John that Hero's maid, Margaret, was his lover, and that she would do anything he demanded. The plan was that Borachio was to make love to Margaret outside Hero's bedroom and to have Don Pedro and Claudio watch from a distance, who would be informed in advance about Hero's disloyalty by Don John. This plan, said Borachio, was to be implemented before the wedding day. He also told Don John that he would make sure Hero was absent when this villainous act was taking place.

Don John promised Borachio a thousand ducats for this plot and asked him to act in a cunning manner. He then set out to find out the day of the wedding.

It was not clear why Don John had taken to conspiracy. The only reason seemed to be his jealousy. Claudio, according to Don John, enjoyed a reputation for being brave and virtuous. This was more than enough for Don John to attempt to make Claudio's life miserable. Conrade and Borachio had agreed to be his accomplices on this mission.

***

Benedick was deep in thought—how disappointed he was that Claudio, who once laughed at other men who had devoted themselves to love, did the very same now. Benedick mused that he would never want to be like Claudio, but he knew fully well the possibility of love transforming him to an oyster. So he resolved to take an oath that until love made an oyster out of him, he would never be such a fool. He would never fall in love unless he found a woman who was beautiful, wise, and virtuous at the same time. Additionally, she should be rich, fair, mild, noble, be able to speak well, and be a good musician.

When Don Pedro, Claudio, Leonato, and Balthasar came out to the garden, Benedick hid in the arbour in order to eavesdrop on their conversation. The men, however, knew that Benedick was in hiding nearby. Don Pedro asked Balthasar to sing the song he had crooned before, and in spite of his reluctance, Balthasar had to break into song, setting a perfect ambience for the ploy that was about to unravel.

*Sigh no more, ladies, sigh no more,*
*Men were deceivers ever,*
*One foot in sea and one on shore,*
*To one thing constant never:*
*Then sigh not so, but let them go,*
*And be you blithe and bonny,*
*Converting all your sounds of woe*
*Into 'Hey nonny, nonny.'*
*Sing no more ditties, sing no more,*
*Of dumps so dull and heavy;*
*The fraud of men was ever so,*
*Since summer first was leafy:*
*Then sigh not so…*

It was time to put Don Pedro's plan into action. Don Pedro asked Leonato if he had really meant it when he had said that Beatrice was in love with Benedick. Leonato and Claudio, who had been instructed earlier, played along, confirming that Beatrice was indeed passionately in love with Benedick and would not tell him for fear of being ridiculed. When Don Pedro suggested that Beatrice might just be pretending, Leonato rejected the idea, saying that Beatrice was too impassioned and tormented for it to be an act. Leonato added that Beatrice, according to Hero, had started writing a letter to Benedick many times in the middle of the night to finally tear it into a thousand shreds. The pranksters painted the picture such that at the end, Leonato expressed his worry that Beatrice might be killed by her melancholia or that she would commit suicide. Hero had believed, Claudio said, that Beatrice would surely kill herself. Benedick easily fell for the ploy after being greatly convinced of the sincerity of the speakers, for among them was an older and well-respected man like Leonato, incapable of low tricks.

When Don Pedro, Claudio, and Leonato left, Benedick exclaimed that he would surely requite Beatrice's love. He said that everything Don Pedro, Claudio, and Leonato had revealed was true and that Beatrice was in fact a fair, virtuous, and witty maid.

When Benedick had told himself the many reasons why he should conceive of marrying Beatrice, Beatrice went in to ask him to join the others for dinner. The transformed Benedick thought that Beatrice's cold invitation had double meanings of love and care.

# 3

To complete the prank, Hero planned to plant the seed of love in Beatrice's ear. With Margaret and Ursula, the two women attending on her, Hero arranged to have Beatrice hear her talking with Ursula about Benedick being madly in love with her.

Margaret was instructed to tell Beatrice that she had overheard Hero and Ursula in conversation and that the subject of their exchange was Beatrice. The plan worked well when Beatrice stealthily hid among the bushes to hear what Hero and Ursula were discussing. Knowing that Beatrice was following their conversation, Hero and Ursula began praising Benedick, saying, 'How wise and handsome he is!'

They slowly took this staged conversation closer to Beatrice's hideout in order that she would not miss any part of their conversation. To add credibility to their tale, Hero mentioned that Beatrice was a self-endeared woman, to which Ursula responded, saying that it was not a wise move to acquaint Beatrice with Benedick's love because it was highly probable that she would make fun of him, just as she always managed to make all men's good qualities look bad.

Behind the bushes, Beatrice was both surprised and moved by Hero and Ursula's comments. In other words, she completely fell victim to their merry scheme. She could hardly believe what she had heard: "What fire is in mine ears? Can this be true? Stand I condemn'd for pride and scorn so much?" At once, however, she said goodbye to maiden pride that came to her very easily in the past. She told herself that she would readily return Benedick's love and even felt the desire to be united with Benedick in holy matrimony.

It seemed that Beatrice was very quick to give in to ideas of love. After having previously established her intense dislike for love and marriage, it was definitely not going to be easy for her to let everyone know her romantic interest in Benedick, let alone Benedick himself. To her advantage, however, Beatrice was intelligent, resourceful, and witty. Maybe she would find a way to ease into the world of love.

***

Don Pedro, Claudio, Leonato, and Benedick were in conversation and Don Pedro told Claudio that he would wait until Claudio's marriage was consummated to head to Aragon. Being the gallant soldier that he was, and a faithful friend to Don Pedro, Claudio at once told Don Pedro that he would accompany him to Aragon. But according to Don Pedro, that would be as bad as giving a child a new coat and keeping him from wearing it. Don Pedro would be satisfied with Benedick's company. In describing Benedick, Don Pedro compared Benedick's heart to a bell and his tongue to the clapper, as he spoke what his heart thought. When Leonato, Claudio, and Don Pedro talked about Benedick's solemn face, Benedick tried to cover up by saying that he was suffering from a toothache. Don Pedro, Claudio, and Leonato knew better as they were the very authors of the prank that was being played on Benedick and Beatrice. While Claudio went on to conjecture that Benedick was in love, Don Pedro, playing his part, said that if Benedick looked sad, it was probably because he was in need of money.

While Don Pedro humoured Benedick and his melancholy disposition, Benedick exclaimed that everyone knew how to overcome an injury except the one who was actually hurt. Claudio insisted that Benedick must be in love, to which Don Pedro joked saying that there was no love in Benedick except for the love of strange costumes. Benedick had recently shaved off his beard, brushed his hat, washed his face, worn cosmetics, and rubbed himself with perfume in order to impress Beatrice. So everyone took to ridiculing Benedick, and soon he excused himself from the gathering and left with Leonato, in order to talk to him in private.

Once Benedick and Leonato were gone, Claudio told Don Pedro that Hero and Margaret had played their part in making Beatrice realise that Benedick was madly in love with her. While Don Pedro was alone with Claudio, Don John came in to speak with his brother in private. He said that Claudio may hear his words as they directly concerned him. Don John's villainous scheme was thus about to materialise.

After verifying that Claudio was about to be married the next day, Don John informed them that Hero was disloyal. He further told them that the world was too trusting of her wicked schemes. Having previously arranged for Borachio to appear at Hero's window, Don John asked Don Pedro and Claudio to wait until the night for evidence of what he had just told them, when they would be able to see Hero's disloyal deeds for themselves.

Even though they were reluctant to take Don John's word for it, both Claudio and Don Pedro agreed that if Don John's report was true, instead of Claudio marrying Hero, they would join forces in bringing disgrace upon her in public. Don John's villainy was thus moving towards fruition, and it would not have been so if not for his willing supporters, Borachio and Conrade. Don John's recent reconciliation with Don Pedro would surely rekindle the prince's fraternal feelings and make him trust his brother. This was, therefore, a perfect time to launch his wicked plot.

# 4

Constable Dogberry, Verges, his deputy, and other watchmen were looking over the city. While they were well-intentioned, their personalities were given to buffoonery and malapropism. Misusing a spate of words to articulate their duties, they would allow thieves to go scot-free and let any man who did not show respect at the mention of Don Pedro, the prince, leave their charge. If babies cried in the night, they agreed to wake up their nurses, and if these nurses would continue to sleep, they would believe it to be their duty to let the nurses sleep till they were woken up by the babies' cries!

The watchmen further agreed that they should sleep rather than make noise, for a noisy watch was intolerable. But Dogberry's words made less sense than what he had perhaps meant to convey: 'To babble and talk is tolerable and not to be endured.' Dogberry instructed the watchmen to get drunkards to bed, and if they did not listen, to leave them alone until they were sober. When it came to handling thieves, Dogberry told Verges that the watchmen should not defile themselves by handling those criminals, and instead let the thieves escape their clutches, thereby establishing their true character. The good-natured, yet ridiculously inept, Dogberry instructed the watch to offend no man and declared that keeping a man against his will was an offence in itself.

Dogberry and Verges left the watch, asking the rest to be 'vigitant' instead of vigilant, and at this instance, the watchmen who had sat down on a church bench to keep watch until two in the morning, came upon a treacherous exchange by Borachio and Conrade. Without knowing that their words were being heard by the watch, Borachio told Conrade how he earned a thousand ducats from John Pedro for a ploy he enacted outside Hero's window. He told Conrade that he made love to Margaret, after having her dress up in Hero's clothes. Underneath the balcony were Claudio and Don Pedro, summoned by Don John Pedro, to witness the staged proof of Hero's disloyalty. When Conrade asked Borachio if 'they' thought that Margaret was Hero, Borachio confirmed that Claudio and Don Pedro did, while Don John Pedro, of course, was well aware of the treacherous scheme.

At this moment, the watchmen who were listening to the entire conversation came forward and arrested Borachio and Conrade. The plot was thus discovered, and it seemed at this point that a suitable end to the vilification that Hero was going to be subjected to was already in the making.

The question remained as to how the villainy that was already under way could be prevented. Don John could already be carrying out his plan. There was very little time to bring the truth to light. The verbosity of Dogberry and Verges was definitely not going to be of any advantage. They took a long time to articulate their intentions, often misusing words and dilly-dallying on trivialities. Would they be able to help prevent Hero from being defamed in public? Were they going to help avoid the misinterpretation of true intentions?

***

On the day of her wedding, Hero woke up early and asked her attendant, Ursula, to wake up Beatrice. As Ursula left to do so, Margaret and Hero were busy choosing dress articles for Hero to wear to church. Margaret mentioned that Hero's wedding gown was ten times better than the gown the Duchess of Milan once wore, complete with gold, lace, pearl, and silver. But Hero's heart was heavy for some reason and she could not lay her finger on what was troubling her. As she confided in Margaret, she teased Hero, saying that she would soon have to bear the weight of a man, which made Hero blush.

When Beatrice arrived and spoke, Hero detected a melancholy trait in her voice. Margaret, aware of the trick that was being played on Beatrice and Benedick, kept hinting that Beatrice was in love with the man. While this was going on, Beatrice informed Hero that she should be ready soon as it was already five in the morning. Beatrice complained of illness, saying that she felt 'stuffed', so Margaret instructed her to get some 'carduus benedictus', hinting clearly at Benedick. But when asked if she had some hidden message in 'benedictus', Margaret vehemently denied any hidden implication.

This is when Ursula came in, informing that the prince, Count Claudio, Benedick, Don John, and all the gallants of the town had come to take Hero to church. Time was short, so Hero earnestly asked Ursula, Margaret, and Beatrice to help her get dressed.

Evil schemes awaited the bride, but Dogberry and Verges were now in the know about Don John's mischief. Would they act quickly enough?

***

Dogberry, the constable, and Verges, his deputy, approached Leonato on the morning of Hero's wedding to inform him of the arrest of Conrade and Borachio. Their tedious and long-winded introduction delayed the communication of the information they had in store for Leonato, who brushed them aside and bade them to examine the suspects themselves.

Using their honest yet misguided and cumbersome expression, Dogberry and Verges took a long time to arrive at the information that was crucial for Leonato. True to his character, Dogberry peppered his speech with all the wrong adjectives.

Dogberry and Verges finally informed Leonato that they had made an arrest and wished to have the criminals examined before Leonato. But again their words came out wrong—instead of saying they had apprehended two suspicious persons, they claimed to have comprehended two auspicious persons. Leonato, in a great hurry to go to church, told the constable and his deputy that he needed to step out, but courteously asked them to drink some wine before they left.

Mixing up their words again, Dogberry and Verges expressed their earnest desire to examine the two suspects dutifully and thoroughly.

Good intentions, it seemed, were not going to be upheld by weak minds. Now that Dogberry and Verges failed to deliver the all too crucial news to Leonato, was Hero going to be vilified as planned? Would Claudio actually defame his love?

# 5

On the morning of the wedding, Don Pedro, Claudio, Don John, Leonato, Friar Francis, and other guests and attendants congregated to perform the ceremony. Leonato instructed the friar to keep the procedures brief. The friar promptly asked Count Claudio if he had come there to marry Hero. To this he answered 'no.' Understanding this to be a joke, Leonato instructed the friar that he had indeed come to be married to her and that it was the friar's task to marry them.

When the friar asked if anyone present had any objections to the imminent marriage, Claudio first asked Hero if she knew any, to which Hero replied, 'none.' When the friar asked Claudio the same question, Leonato answered in the negative on his behalf, saying, 'I dare make his answer, none.' Count Claudio's cryptic response was 'O, what men dare do! What men may do! What men daily do, not knowing what they do!' meaning that men often perform unthinkable deeds assuming falsely that what they believe is true. Count Claudio, after being tricked into believing Hero was disloyal, asked Leonato to take her back as she was an immodest and lascivious woman who entertained men in her bedroom late at night: 'There, Leonato, take her back again: Give not this rotten orange to your friend.' Claudio further added that Hero's modest appearance was simply a guise and that she had no modesty, knowing the "heat of a luxurious bed". Leonato asked the count if he meant that the couple had already consummated their marriage, to which Claudio responded, saying that his love towards Hero had been of a brotherly kind thus far, denying the existence of physical relations. He went on to chide Hero, accusing her of maintaining the appearance of Diane, the goddess of chastity, while she was really an amorous Venus in nature. As Claudio heaped accusations on Hero, Leonato entreated the prince to interfere on their behalf. Don Pedro, however, had already been fooled by Don John into witnessing the staged scene of amorous love between Hero and a stranger when indeed it had been Margaret wearing Hero's clothes with Borachio at Hero's window. Don Pedro, therefore, had no words of comfort for Leonato. He only expressed his extreme displeasure in Leonato's attempt to join his friend's hand in marriage with a wanton woman.

Leonato was greatly distressed to hear such a vile testimony of his only daughter's wantonness. While he was overcome with disbelief, Claudio said that he would pose one question to Hero and that Leonato should exercise his fatherly and kindly power to make her answer truthfully. Claudio's question was this: who was the man she had conversed with between twelve and one the night before outside her bedroom window? The bewildered Hero replied that she had not been with any man during that hour, and Don Pedro at once said that she was no maiden, and that he had seen her outside her window with a stranger, who had confessed that they had had such 'vile encounters' a thousand times before.

Don John interjected, saying that those encounters were not to be named. He told Hero that he was sorry for her misgovernment. Leonato, of course, was absolutely devastated, and when he asked for a dagger to take his own life, Hero fainted, the shock of the morning's turn of events being too much for her to bear. Concluding that the recent events had smothered Hero's spirits, Don John left with the prince and Claudio, leaving behind an unhappy gathering.

Now everyone, especially Beatrice, focused their attention on the fainted Hero. While the friar, Beatrice, and Benedick were concerned about Hero's well-being, Leonato, her father, expressed his strong inclination to have her dead rather than alive, for she had been a disgraceful daughter. Leonato was so angry, hurt, and ashamed that he vowed to kill her himself. He vehemently disowned her, claiming that no part of her was derived from his loins.

Benedick attempted to mitigate Leonato's anger and frustration by asking him to be patient. He himself was shocked at the morning's turn of events. Beatrice was greatly shaken by the injustice her cousin had been subjected to and claimed that Hero had been cruelly belied. Taking this as a cue, Benedick asked Beatrice if she had been Hero's bedfellow the night before, and even though Beatrice said that she had not, she added that she had indeed been so for an entire period of twelve months before. The unappeasable Leonato intervened at this point and exclaimed aloud that the report of Hero's immodesty had been confirmed. Like a drowning man who clutches at a straw, Leonato was swift to find the prince's and Claudio's words reliable, especially given their stature as well as Claudio's love for Hero. It was impossible, in his words, for them to devise a treacherous scheme having Hero's interest at heart.

The friar, however, was convinced that a grave error had taken place. But Leonato maintained that it was unlikely and that Hero's only hope to not damn herself any further was by not adding perjury to her damnation.

When the friar questioned Hero regarding the identity of the man she had been accused of having entertained at her bedroom window, Hero answered that she had absolutely no idea, and that if there was indeed such a man, only her accusers would know of him. Benedick was quick to add that while the prince and Claudio had the zeal of honour, it was the prince's bastard brother whose efforts had resulted in such a villainy.

The friar entreated Leonato to listen to his counsel, on grounds that a huge misunderstanding had taken place. Since the prince and Claudio had taken their leave of Hero after her vilification, the friar instructed everyone present to maintain that Hero was dead and to further carry out this deception by mounting epitaphs on the family's old monument and performing all rites that pertained to a burial. The friar surmised that news of her sudden and unexpected death would transform the hearts of her accusers to make them feel sorry for her after the cause of her death—their slanderous accusations—would fill them with repentance. 'The news would surely quench the shock of her infamy,' declared the friar. The friar further said that people don't value the things they have until they lose them, when they suddenly wake up to all the virtues they were blind to when they were alive. That's how Claudio would also respond; when he would hear that she had died from his words, his imagination would be filled with sweet thoughts of her. Then, if he ever truly loved her, he would mourn her and wish he hadn't accused her—even though he believed his accusation to be true. If by any chance things did not turn out the way the friar envisioned, he instructed Leonato to hide Hero and have her commit to a reclusive and religious life.

Everyone present pledged their secrecy. Her wedding day had only just been prolonged, the friar hoped, and he, Leonato, and Hero went their separate ways, leaving Beatrice and Benedick to each other.

The time was ripe for Beatrice and Benedick to confess their love for each other after the perfect working of the plot woven by their friends. With uncharacteristic candour, they exchanged thoughts of love. 'Tell me what I can do for you,' Benedick asked Beatrice. 'Kill Claudio,' was Beatrice's quick reply. But Benedick's refusal was as instantaneous. So Beatrice bade him goodbye, saying that denying her was the same as killing her. Benedick, however, was persistent in his plea to detain Beatrice further to find an answer for the plight she was in. When he asked Beatrice if Claudio was her enemy, she, in return, asked Benedick if someone who slandered and dishonoured her kinswoman was indeed not: "Is he not approved in the height a villain, that hath slandered, scorned, dishonoured my kinswoman?" She wished she was a man so that she could rip his heart out in public. She said that she hated Claudio all the more because he had pretended that everything was fine until the moment he was supposed to exchange vows with Claudio.

After Benedick refused to kill Claudio for a second time, Beatrice repeated that she wanted to be a man or have a friend who would be a man for her sake! She angrily remarked that there were no real men left. Their manliness had been reduced to pretty curtsies and fancy manners, and their bravery consisted of making clever compliments. Benedick asked Beatrice if she thought that Count Claudio had wronged Hero, she answered with absolute surety. Beatrice had given him her affirmation, and now Benedick said that he would challenge Claudio. He swore that Claudio would pay dearly for his rash accusation. He asked Beatrice to console Hero and left to take care of the matter at hand.

***

In the meantime, Dogberry, Verges and the rest of the watch met with the sexton for the trial of the previously arrested Borachio and Conrade. In keeping with his ludicrous quality, Dogberry continued to misuse words. When the sexton asked who the malefactors were, Dogberry claimed that he was the one, mistaking, of course, malefactor for benefactor.

Dogberry asked the sexton to write everything down. Both Borachio and Conrade vehemently denied that they were false knaves. The sexton told Dogberry that he was going about the examination the wrong way and that he should call their accusers. Dogberry agreed that it was the quickest way to proceed.

Now the watchmen chimed in and accused Borachio and Conrade of calling Don Pedro's brother a villain and accepting a thousand ducats from him for accusing Lady Hero wrongfully. The watch further added that Count Claudio, having accepted the tale, intended to disgrace Lady

Hero in front of the gathering and not marry her.

After Borachio and Conrade were accused of these charges, the sexton told everyone that Don John had secretly stolen away from Messina that morning and that Hero had been accused falsely, just as the watchmen said. He added that Hero had also suddenly died, unable to bear the unexpected grief. Dogberry then asked Borachio and Conrade to be 'opinioned'. What he meant, though, was for them to be 'pinioned'.

Had the truth come to light too late? The truth was in the hands of seemingly inept men, no matter their good intentions. Beatrice had resolved to do justice by her cousin, the gallant Benedick had vowed to aid her, but the powerful prince had been hoodwinked. How could order be restored in this world?

# 6

Antonio said to his brother, Leonato, that if he went on grieving about Hero, he would ultimately kill himself: "If you go on thus, you will kill yourself. And 'tis not wisdom thus to second grief against yourself." Leonato, however, asked not to be given advice. He told Antonio that any man could counsel another when he himself did not suffer such a loss. His grief, Leonato continued, was not something any advice could mitigate. But to Antonio, his brother seemed childish. He paid no heed to his statement and advised Leonato not to hold himself completely responsible for Hero's infamy. Instead, Leonato should make the offenders suffer too, he said.

At this point, Claudio and Don Pedro happened to go past the two brothers. Even though they pretended to be in a hurry, Leonato arrested their attention and accused Claudio of doing him wrong. Claudio's hand went to his sword, but Leonato was not daunted. He accused Claudio of falsely accusing his innocent child and thereby causing her death. When Leonato accused Claudio of villainy, the accused was baffled and asked for clarification. Don Pedro quickly took Claudio's side and charged Leonato with lying: "I stand dishonour'd, that have gone about to link my dear friend to a common stale." As the argument grew hotter, Leonato challenged Claudio to a duel, which the latter refused, saying, 'I will not do with you.'

Claudio thus avoided Leonato, but now Antonio joined in, challenging Claudio to a duel. Despite Leonato's interjections, Antonio continued to insult and challenge Claudio. Don Pedro interfered and told both Leonato and Antonio that he was sorry for Hero's death but her death was caused by an undeniable and proven truth: "Gentlemen both, we will not wake your patience. My heart is sorry for your daughter's death: But, on my honour, she was charged with nothing but what was true and very full of proof."

Though Leonato continued to address the prince, Don Pedro said that he would not hear him. Finally, taking this cue, Leonato went away with his brother.

At this point Benedick arrived, seeking Claudio and Don Pedro, who said that they were looking for Benedick as well. Don Pedro told Benedick that he and Claudio were in a melancholy mood and were looking for him so he could ease their spirits with his merry and witty demeanour.

It slowly dawned on both Don Pedro and Claudio that Benedick was in a very serious mood. In private, he called

Claudio a villain who had caused an innocent lady's death and challenged him to a duel, which Claudio readily accepted. They were to meet for the duel the next day. Telling Don Pedro that he wished to discontinue being in his company, Benedick left. As a parting thought, he added that Don Pedro's brother had fled Messina. At this point there was no questioning Benedick's seriousness. Don Pedro and Claudio concluded that Benedick's behaviour was caused by his love for Beatrice.

It seemed that the prince and Claudio, however well-intentioned they may have been, were somewhat peeved by Benedick's behaviour. It was very strange that friendship could be so easily forgotten. Stranger still for a man like Claudio, who was ruled by love, to think that Benedick's irrational behaviour was caused by love. Was Benedick a fool to challenge his good friend? Was Claudio a fool to accept it? Was the prince weak to see it happen without opposing it?

At this moment, Dogberry and Verges arrived at the scene with their watch. And so did Borachio and Conrade. Don Pedro noticed at once that two of his brother's men were bound. And soon he was frustrated by Dogberry's long-winded explanations. He asked Borachio what their offence was. Borachio confessed the whole villainous scheme he had taken part in: under Don John's prompting, he had slandered Hero. It was Margaret dressed in Hero's clothes that Don Pedro and Claudio had seen at Hero's window, and Hero had died as a result of this treacherous scheme.

Claudio and Don Pedro were devastated by the new revelations. Dogberry mentioned to them that by this time the sexton would have informed (he mistakenly said 'reformed') Leonato of the news, and no sooner had he spoken than Leonato and the sexton approached the gathering. When Claudio and Don Pedro begged his forgiveness and offered themselves up willingly to any punishment that Leonato had in mind, Leonato said that he simply wanted a few practical matters fulfilled: he wanted them to inform the people of Messina that Hero had been wrongly accused; he wanted Claudio to hang epitaphs on her tomb and sing them to the corpse, and finally he wanted him to marry his brother's daughter who was almost identical to Leonato's presumably dead child. Claudio thanked Leonato for the mercy he had shown him, and after inviting Claudio to his place the following day, Leonato turned to Borachio. He mentioned that Borachio should be brought face to face with Margaret who had taken part in this plot, but Borachio admitted that Margaret had had no hand in the matter at all and had always been just and virtuous.

When the matter had been thus cleared, Leonato left Don Pedro and Claudio, reminding them that they would meet the next morning. Don Pedro promised that they would not fail him, and Claudio expressed his resolve to mourn for Hero that night.

***

Benedick showered compliments on Margaret in order to win her favour and thereby gain access to Beatrice. Margaret readily flirted with Benedick but soon left to call Beatrice. In her absence, Benedick lamented that he was not good at writing poetry. When Beatrice finally arrived, the two lovers flirted with each other freely. Their words had a slight edge of friendly hostility, but they were governed by love. Benedick told Beatrice that he had challenged Claudio.

While Beatrice and Benedick engaged in a flirtatious exchange, Ursula, Beatrice's attendant, arrived in haste to let them know that the unjustness of the accusations, which had been hurled at Hero, had come to light and that Claudio and Don Pedro had been mightily abused. Ursula asked Beatrice to go to her uncles to witness the affair and Beatrice asked Benedick if he would join her to hear the details. Benedick replied with a witty rejoinder, saying that he would live in her heart, die in her lap, be buried in her eyes, and furthermore, go with her to her uncles.

***

Meanwhile, Claudio and the prince, along with several attendants and Balthasar, visited Leonato's monument. Claudio read from a scroll an epitaph he had written for Hero. When he had finished reading the epitaph, Balthasar sang.

*Pardon, goddess of the night,*
*Those that slew thy virgin knight;*
*For the which, with songs of woe,*

*Round about her tomb they go.*
*Midnight, assist our moan;*
*Help us to sigh and groan,*
*Heavily, heavily:*
*Graves, yawn and yield your dead,*
*Till death be uttered,*
*Heavily, heavily.*

Claudio hung the epitaph on Hero's supposed grave. This was one of the promises he had made to Leonato and now fulfilled as punishment for his false accusations. After completing this task, Claudio asked everyone to go their own way but to meet at Leonato's for the wedding ceremony where he was to marry Antonio's daughter, who supposedly looked just like Hero. The wedding was to take place later that same day.

***

A happy group that consisted of Leonato and his brother, the friar, Hero, Benedick, Ursula, Margaret and other attendants, prepared themselves to welcome the prince and Claudio who was to marry Hero's supposed cousin. Everyone was prepared to play their part. Benedick asked Leonato for the hand of his niece, Beatrice, in marriage. Both Leonato and the friar gave their blessings and they saw that the prince and Claudio were approaching with other attendants. This is when Leonato asked Antonio to summon his daughter. Soon Antonio came back with Hero, Beatrice,

Ursula, Margaret, and other ladies, all masked.

When Claudio wanted to see his bride's face, Leonato rejected the request, saying he wouldn't allow it until Claudio took her hand and, in front of the friar, swore to marry her. When Claudio did as told and unmasked Hero, he made no mistake in recognising her and was shocked, to say the least. The friar quickly cleared the confusion. Leonato clarified that Hero was only dead as long as her slander lived. Both of them were happy to have found each other again. It was then that Benedick unmasked Beatrice. When he asked her in public if she loved him, she said she did not! When Beatrice asked the same of Benedick, he said he did not either. But Claudio and Hero merrily reported an effusion of love, unveiling sonnets they had written to each other, leaving no doubt in anyone's mind that they were in love.

Benedick and Beatrice started their merry war again, but this time, Benedick stopped Beatrice by kissing her. Don Pedro asked Benedick how it felt to be a married man. Benedict said that no amount of wisecracks could dampen his mood. He didn't care what people called him or thought of him—he was not afraid. Since he had decided to get married, he wouldn't hear anyone say a bad thing about it. He asked them not to make fun of his previous views on marriage any more. He concluded that men were impulsive beings. Claudio and Benedick, whose friendship had been rekindled, humoured each other and Benedick proposed the idea of having a dance before they were married. Even though Leonato said they could have the dancing after the wedding, Benedick went ahead with his original plan and asked the musicians to start playing. A messenger entered at this point and informed everyone that Don John had been arrested while attempting to flee and had been brought to Messina by armed men. Benedick said that they could devise punishments for the offenders later, but for now, he asked the pipers to play music.

Benedick's last words confirmed the mirth of the situation when he said, "Come, come, we are friends: let's have a dance ere we are married, that we may lighten our own hearts and our wives' heels." So good prevailed and the malevolent plotter would be punished.

Hero and Claudio were rightfully united; and of course, Beatrice and Benedick, too.

Messina was a happy place once again.

# Supplementary Reading

# Character Sketches

## BEATRICE

Beatrice is niece to Leonato, the governor of Messina. It is quite evident that she is very clever with words. While Beatrice and Hero, her cousin, are friends and bedfellows, Beatrice is more assertive, confident about her intentions, and displays strength of character in the face of adversity. This is quite different from Hero, who epitomises feminine charm, grace, and obedience.

Beatrice commands the respect of her attendants and the love and adoration of her elders, including her uncle, Leonato. Even though she's swift and witty with words, she acts differently towards her elders. When it comes to Benedick, however, Beatrice is feisty, overly witty, and almost vitriolic. As Leonato himself explains, the witty banter between Beatrice and Benedick should not be held against her charm and character. Whenever she meets Benedick, they attack each other with words and almost always compete, trying to outwit the other.

The merry scheme that Don Pedro comes up with

for Beatrice and Benedick to fall in love with each other introduces us to a malleable, feminine, and graceful side of Beatrice. Even though initially she completely rejects any romantic advances from the opposite sex and maintains complete independence, when she hears (as planned by Don Pedro) that Benedick is in love with her, she sheds her guard very readily. It almost makes one think that Beatrice simply needed a man, a lover, to tame her overconfident, aggressive, and almost militant nature. Though she tries to outwit Benedick at every turn, when she decides to love him, she completely gives herself in. In fact, when she first overhears Hero and Ursula talking about Benedick's feelings for her, she immediately tells herself that she would return his love.

Even though she readily accepts Benedick's love, Beatrice is also extremely loyal to her kith and kin. When Hero is falsely accused by Claudio and Don Pedro, she is utterly saddened at her cousin's plight and is bitterly angered by the perpetrators, so much so that when Benedick asks her what he can do for her, she immediately asks for Claudio to be murdered. The strength of her character is evident in the way she handles Hero's plight. Comforting her cousin with compassionate and loving words, Beatrice at the same time, expresses how she would love to be a man to avenge this misdeed. Beatrice refuses to adhere to the socially accepted gender role of her time, but also wishes to be a man in order to set things right. In a sense then, Beatrice is trapped by her patriarchal system; however, at the same time, she is not easily satisfied or silenced by the system.

## BENEDICK

Benedick is a charming character. Having just returned from the wars along with Don Pedro and Claudio, he, just like Beatrice, rejects love. From the beginning it becomes very clear that Benedick is a source of entertainment. We get the first glimpse of this attribute when he banters with Beatrice. A valiant soldier, Benedick decidedly refuses to be charmed by feminine graces. He is forsworn to love.

This only proves a myth, however, and very soon, clearly falling into the trap that Don Pedro has woven for him, he falls in love with Beatrice, and no longer does he express his affinity to independence and the mockery of female vile behaviour. In fact, it takes hardly any time for Benedick to requite the love that Beatrice has (supposedly) professed for him. The gallant, masculine, chauvinistic Benedick undergoes a profound change of character upon falling in love with Beatrice. He becomes peaceful, mellower, and better-behaved. In fact, he even flirts with Ursula in order to gain access to Beatrice. This profound character change also manifests in his physical persona. He shaves off his beard, which not only testifies that he has fallen in love, but that he has also revised his gender role, the beard standing for masculinity and authority.

Benedick, like Beatrice, displays the strong and praiseworthy attribute of loyalty to friends. After he has fallen in love with Beatrice and Hero has been falsely accused, Beatrice asks Benedick to kill Claudio. His instantaneous answer is that he will not. This is a wonderful moment in the play in which his strong and unshakeable loyalty to his friends comes to the surface. After having completely succumbed to the idea of falling in love with Beatrice, he has the conviction to not let an old friendship suffer. Unlike Beatrice, however, Benedick's conviction is only short-lived. In order to appease Beatrice and safeguard his role in the love affair, he gradually succumbs to Beatrice's wishes and challenges Claudio to a duel. Once convinced by Beatrice, he even goes a step further and tells the prince that he must forswear the prince's company.

When the play seems to be steering towards a tragic end, Benedick becomes almost sinister in his threats to Claudio, formerly his best friend. Inspired by his love for Beatrice, he has clearly fitted himself into the patriarchal role of the chivalrous knight. When the confusions instigated by Don John come to light and the play ends happily, we see a happy Benedick, too, united with his lady love. We must remember though, he will go to any lengths to protect his woman in the face of adversity.

## DON PEDRO

The prince of Aragon, Don Pedro, is clearly the most powerful character in the play. Even Leonato, the governor of Messina, is under his power. Though Claudio and Benedick are friends, they too find him formidable. Don Pedro is held in great respect by Leonato, who happens to be an old friend of his.

When Claudio confides in the prince about his love interest in Hero, the prince undertakes to woo her for Claudio. This is a highly questionable proposition. Why could he not let Claudio woo Hero himself? The prince comes across as a benevolent character; however, it seems that his decisions are arbitrary and almost unethical. If, for instance, Hero did not like Claudio, what would her plight be? Because it was the prince who wooed on Claudio's behalf, does she have to accept him anyway, irrespective of her preferences?

Don Pedro proposes to Beatrice, even though it comes across as a joke in the play. The proposal is brushed aside as nothing but that. The prince does not pursue the cause, but at the end of the play, Benedick points out that Don Pedro looks sad. Could Don Pedro be sad because Beatrice is marrying Benedick?

Also curious are Don Pedro's interactions with his friends, especially Leonato. When Leonato entreats to be heard, Don Pedro refuses to hear him. It seems then that old friendships (and by extension, friends who are old by years) matter less to him than friends who are young. Don Pedro seems very close to Claudio, more so than to Benedick.

Don Pedro's character is somewhat equivocal and unlike other characters in the play, we are presented with very little information about him. Whatever his real motives might be, he does use his authority towards positive ends. His relationship with Don John is intriguing. Again we are not given any facts, but we could conclude that Don Pedro is somewhat loyal to his illegitimate brother after they have made amends.

Don Pedro, unlike other characters in the play, is enigmatic and therefore open to varying interpretations.

# Questions

## 1

- Why were Benedick and Beatrice always trying to outwit or compete with each other? Were they enemies?
- Why couldn't Claudio propose to Hero himself? Was Don Pedro's plan ethical?
- Why was Don John always trying to cause trouble? What is his role in the story?
- Messengers seem to carry important roles in this story. How reliable is their information?
- Is Leonato a good man, a good father? Why do you think so?

## 2

- Why was Beatrice forsworn to love?
- What messages circulated at the masquerade ball? How did characters use masks to confuse, mislead, and frustrate others?
- What was the plot Borachio proposed to Don John? What was his reward?
- What was the trick played on Benedick? Was it successful?
- Do you agree that Beatrice is fair, virtuous, and witty? Why or why not?

## 3

- What was the trick played on Beatrice? Was it successful?
- What did Don John tell Claudio and Don Pedro? Did they believe him?
- What did the watch discover? Why was it important?
- Why was Beatrice not feeling well on Hero's wedding day?
- Why were Dogberry and Verges tedious with their words? What could have happened if they weren't?

## 4

- What happened at the wedding?
- Was Leonato's response reasonable? Why did he behave that way?
- Was Benedick's initial answer to Beatrice's question (about killing Claudio) reasonable? What does it say about his character?
- What were the results of the hearing?
- Was the friar's plan effective? Why or why not?

## 5

- Is Antonio a good brother? Is Leonato's behaviour reasonable, excessive, or blame-worthy?
- Is Benedick blinded by love? Is Claudio a villain?
- What is Leonato's ultimate plan?
- Why is Don Pedro somewhat sad at the end of the play?
- Could this story have been tragic? What changes need to be made to the story to make it a tragedy?

## WHO WAS SHAKESPEARE?

William Shakespeare (1564-1616) was an English poet and playwright. He is now widely regarded as one of the greatest writers in the English language and the greatest playwright of all time.

Shakespeare was baptised on 26 April 1564 in Stratford-Upon-Avon. His father John was a glovemaker and dealer in wool. His mother Mary was the daughter of a prosperous farmer. They had eight children.

In 1582, Shakespeare married Anne Hathaway. They had three children, Susanna, Hamnet and Judith.

Little is known about Shakespeare until 1592. At this time, records show that he was living in London and writing poetry. His early plays were also written during this period.

In 1592, Shakespeare became a founding member, actor and playwright of Lord Chamberlain's Men, a theatre company. The most famous actor in this company was Richard Burbage, who played the roles of Richard III and King Lear. This company was later renamed as King's Men.

Little else is known about Shakespeare's life, though he clearly earned a lot of money for his plays. He became a substantial landowner.

He died in 1616, and was buried in Stratford.

In 1623, two actors from the King's Men had Shakespeare's plays published in what is now called the *First Folio*. This contained thirty-six plays and was sold for £1.

The period during which Shakespeare lived and wrote is now called the Elizabethan age, the reign of Queen Elizabeth I (1533-1603), during which many great playwrights, such as Christopher Marlowe and Ben Jonson wrote.

The works of Shakespeare that survive include 38 plays, 154 sonnets and two long narrative poems. Shakespeare's plays have been translated into every major language, read, performed on stage and made into films, and continue to inspire new interpretations all around the world even today.

## WHY READ SHAKESPEARE?

'Shakespeare's work is the fullest expression of the dilemmas that we as humans face ... he's capable of seeing two sides of a situation so there's always drama and there's always conflict.'—Michael Boyd, RSC Artistic Director.

Shakespeare is still read and loved because his plays contain fabulous stories, wonderful characters and are full of marvellous poetry.

Shakespeare's plays are best watched first and then read, because in performance they take on a new magic. Today many filmmakers are making films on Shakespeare's plays. You can try watching them to get a sense of how the plays would be in performance.

## PLAYS AND THE THEATRE IN SHAKESPEARE'S TIME

Performances in Elizabethan theatres were very different from when you go to see a play now. The actors and the audience always interacted. Shakespeare's company had to perform against the noise of the crowd which shouted, threw fruits and tried to join the actors on stage.

Unlike the playwrights of today, writers like Shakespeare would have to present their theatre company with their ideas. The leading actors and managers would decide whether they liked them or not, and only then could the playwright proceed. This close relationship meant that the playwrights often wrote roles with a particular actor in mind.

When a play was completed, actors would receive only their lines, and not the whole play. Thus, until rehearsals started, they would not have any idea how the parts would fit together to form a cohesive play. Rehearsals were used to sort out all the details not mentioned in the script, such as songs, exits and on-stage actions.

The Elizabethan stage was different from the proscenium stage we see in theatres nowadays. The cheaper tickets were for the groundlings, the audience on three sides of the stage. The more expensive tickets were for patrons who sat in covered seats further back. The stage was covered in straw. The wall at the back had three entrances. Above the stage was a trapdoor for lowering performers down to the stage, and on the stage itself was another trapdoor for surprise entrances and exits.